LADY'S MAN

The man brought up his fist and hit the woman in the face, knocking her against the bar. Fargo strode across the room to the bar, where the man had drawn back his fist to strike another blow. He started to swing.

Fargo's hand closed around his wrist, stopping the blow in midair. The man's head jerked toward him, his mouth contorting in a snarl. "Who the hell—"

Fargo started to squeeze. The man gasped as bones grated together in his wrist. "That's no way to treat a lady, hombre," Fargo said.

The man's other hand plucked a knife from a sheath at his waist. With a curse, he thrust the blade at Fargo's belly. . . .

THE TRAILSMAN

#293

OZARK BLOOD FEUD

by

Jon Sharpe

A SIGNET BOOK

SIGNET
Published by New American Library, a division of
Penguin Group (USA) Inc., 375 Hudson Street,
New York, New York 10014, USA
Penguin Group (Canada), 90 Eglinton Avenue East, Suite 700, Toronto,
Ontario M4P 2Y3, Canada (a division of Pearson Penguin Canada Inc.)
Penguin Books Ltd., 80 Strand, London WC2R 0RL, England
Penguin Ireland, 25 St. Stephen's Green, Dublin 2,
Ireland (a division of Penguin Books Ltd.)
Penguin Group (Australia), 250 Camberwell Road, Camberwell, Victoria 3124,
Australia (a division of Pearson Australia Group Pty. Ltd.)
Penguin Books India Pvt. Ltd., 11 Community Centre, Panchsheel Park,
New Delhi - 110 017, India
Penguin Group (NZ), cnr Airborne and Rosedale Roads, Albany,
Auckland 1310, New Zealand (a division of Pearson New Zealand Ltd.)
Penguin Books (South Africa) (Pty.) Ltd., 24 Sturdee Avenue,
Rosebank, Johannesburg 2196, South Africa

Penguin Books Ltd., Registered Offices:
80 Strand, London WC2R 0RL, England

First published by Signet, an imprint of New American Library,
a division of Penguin Group (USA) Inc.

First Printing, March 2006
10 9 8 7 6 5 4 3 2 1

The first chapter of this book previously appeared in *San Francisco Showdown*, the two hundred ninety-second volume in this series.

Copyright © Penguin Group (USA) Inc., 2006
All rights reserved

 REGISTERED TRADEMARK—MARCA REGISTRADA

The Trailsman

Beginnings . . . they bend the tree and they mark the man. Skye Fargo was born when he was eighteen. Terror was his midwife, vengeance his first cry. Killing spawned Skye Fargo, ruthless, cold-blooded murder. Out of the acrid smoke of gunpowder still hanging in the air, he rose, cried out a promise never forgotten.

The Trailsman they began to call him all across the West: searcher, scout, hunter, the man who could see where others only looked, his skills for hire but not his soul, the man who lived each day to the fullest, yet trailed each tomorrow. Skye Fargo, the Trailsman, the seeker who could take the wildness of a land and the wanting of a woman and make them his own.

The Ozark Mountains of Missouri, 1860—
where the chilly winds of winter are no colder
than the hearts of evil men.

= 1 =

The big man in buckskins and a sheepskin jacket tugged his hat down tighter on his head and gritted his teeth against the bite of the wind. His lake blue eyes squinted. He was riding north, into the blustery gusts, and he didn't like it.

Neither did the magnificent black-and-white stallion. The Ovaro tossed his head and nickered as if to ask what they were doing out in weather like this. He ought to be in a warm stable somewhere, and his rider needed to be inside, too, preferably with a hot meal in his belly.

That wasn't likely to happen any time soon, Skye Fargo told himself. He wasn't sure how far it was to the next place where he could find shelter.

The late-afternoon sky was choked with thick gray clouds. The light of day was fading fast. The landscape was made even more dismal by the thickly wooded hills that loomed on both sides of the twisting road Fargo followed.

He had planned on reaching the settlement of Bear Creek by nightfall, but it looked like that wasn't going to happen. He would have to either push on after dark, or find a farm where he could spend the night.

The trail led through a little valley with a small stream at the bottom. As cold as it was, there would be ice on the edges of that creek by the next morning. The Ovaro's hooves rang on the crude bridge that crossed it. Fargo started up the slope on the northern side of the valley.

He reined in sharply. A frown creased his forehead as he stared up the road at the top of the hill.

Several figures were walking down the slope toward him. Fargo couldn't see them that well in the fading light, and they were shapeless because they appeared to be bundled up in heavy coats. He started to count. There were seven of them, and several of them were small.

Probably a family, thought Fargo as he rubbed the close-cropped dark beard on his jaw. The little ones would be kids. What were they doing out walking around on a frigid day like this?

He nudged the stallion into motion and headed up the hill toward the pilgrims. They didn't seem to notice him. They walked with heads down and shoulders hunched, trying to stay warm, and since the wind was behind them, they evidently didn't hear the Ovaro's hoofbeats until Fargo had almost reached them.

Then the figure in the lead stopped short, yelled in alarm, and took a hurried step backward. He reached under his coat and brought out a gun. It was an old flintlock pistol, but at this range it could be as deadly as any modern weapon.

"Don't come any closer! I'll shoot. I swear it!"

Fargo reined the Ovaro to a halt. The voice that had called the warning was high-pitched, probably not that of a woman but more likely a boy. The barrel of the old pistol shook, but whether that was from the cold or the nerves of the person holding it, Fargo didn't know. Probably some of both.

"Take it easy, son," Fargo said calmly. He didn't want to spook the boy into pulling the trigger. The youngster was trembling so much he would probably miss, but there was no point in taking chances. Fargo went on. "I'm a friend."

"The hell, you say." The boy probably hoped the profanity made him sound older. "We ain't got no friends in this neck of the woods."

"Well, I'm not an enemy, anyway," Fargo said. "Couldn't be, because I never saw you before."

Now that the boy was standing straighter and looking up at the man on the horse, Fargo could see his face better. It was pale and drawn, haggard with strain. The boy's nose was red and running from the cold. He looked scared out of his wits.

That didn't make him any less dangerous, of course. As long as he pointed that pistol at Fargo, he was a threat.

The others had come to a stop behind the boy and now huddled together in the road. One of them was a little taller than the boy with the gun. The rest were smaller.

"Calvin, be careful," said the taller one. Definitely a female voice this time, Fargo noted, and fairly young. "Don't shoot unless you have to."

"You don't have to tell me what to do, Junie," the boy snapped. "I got this under control."

He was so far from having the situation under control that it was sort of sad, but Fargo didn't point that out. Instead he asked, "Who are you folks, and why are you walking?"

"How else are you gonna get somewhere when you ain't got no wagon nor mules?" Calvin said. "We ain't lookin' for trouble, mister, so move aside and we'll be on our way."

"Where are you bound?"

"That's none of your business."

The sharp answer didn't surprise Fargo. Calvin

3

wasn't the least bit friendly. Or maybe he was just so scared that he had put up a wall around him and wasn't going to let anybody else in.

The young woman spoke up again. "We're heading for Springfield."

Calvin jerked his head toward her. "Damn it, Junie. Don't be tellin' this stranger anything! You know we can't trust nobody!"

Fargo could have urged the Ovaro forward while Calvin wasn't looking and ridden right over him. Fargo wasn't too worried anymore about the youngster being able to hit anything with that old horse pistol. He wasn't even convinced that the ancient weapon would actually fire.

But he stayed where he was, figuring he could do more good for these hapless pilgrims if he got them to trust him. He said, "I'm not looking for trouble, either. I'm bound for Jefferson City. Got a job waiting for me there."

"Jefferson City's a long way," Junie said.

"So's Springfield," Fargo pointed out. "Must be sixty, seventy miles from here." He had passed through the town several days earlier on his way north from Arkansas.

"Closer to eighty," the young woman said.

Calvin was getting frustrated. "Damn it. Will you stop talkin' to this fella?" he burst out. "We got to keep movin'! You know that."

"You plan on walking all the way to Springfield?" Fargo asked.

Junie nodded. She had a scarf wrapped around her head. A few tendrils of blond hair strayed out from under it. "We don't have any choice. Like my brother said, we don't have a wagon or any mules to pull one."

So they were brother and sister. Fargo wondered if the smaller ones were their siblings, too. They watched

4

Fargo with wide eyes. He could see now that some of them were wrapped up in threadbare blankets, rather than bundled in coats.

"You can't walk that far in the middle of winter."

"Are you deaf, mister?" Calvin asked rudely. "Ain't nothin' else we can do."

"Don't you have a home?"

A couple of the little ones began to cry. When that happened, Fargo knew he had hit on something.

As Junie tried to comfort the ones who were crying and get them to hush, Fargo said, "That's it, isn't it? You don't have a home."

"We got kinfolks in Springfield," Calvin said. "I reckon they'll take us in."

"But there's nowhere else you can go, so you have to walk halfway across Missouri in the dead of winter."

"We'll be fine." An edge of hysteria crept into Calvin's voice. Fargo guessed his pride wouldn't let him admit, even to himself, what a bad situation they were really in.

He nodded toward the little ones. "Are those your brothers and sisters?"

"You leave us alone," Calvin said thinly. "Don't you even think about takin' them away, or splittin' us up—"

"I'm not going to split anybody up," Fargo said. "But maybe I can help you—"

"No! There's nothin' anybody can do!"

One of the children suddenly gave a wail. "Calvin, I wanna go home!" she sobbed.

The boy spun toward her. "Shut up!" he cried raggedly. "Hush up that bawlin'!"

Junie put her arms around the smaller girl. "Calvin, stop it!" she scolded. "Hannah can't help it. She's worn-out and half-frozen like the rest of us."

5

She might be more than half-frozen before morning. Night was coming on soon, and the temperature would drop even more once darkness fell. And Fargo hadn't passed any place in the last ten miles where these children could take shelter.

This had gone on long enough. He swung down from the saddle.

Calvin must have heard him dismount. The boy whirled back around and started to bring the old pistol up. "I told you to leave us alone—" he began.

Fargo stepped forward swiftly, closed his hand around the barrel of the pistol, and yanked it out of Calvin's grasp. He moved past the angrily sputtering boy and handed the gun to Junie.

"I reckon I can trust *you* not to shoot me?"

She took the pistol, and then Fargo bent to gather the girl called Hannah into his arms. She was seven or eight, with a couple of reddish-blond braids sticking out from under the blanket that was pulled over her head.

Fargo picked her up, cradling her against his broad, muscular chest, and told her, "You don't have to cry, honey. Everything's going to be all right."

"Don't tell her that!" Calvin shouted behind him. "You don't know that!" He sounded like he was about to start crying himself.

"Mister," Junie said quietly, "who are you?"

"My name is Skye Fargo. Like I told you, I'm on my way to Jefferson City."

"That's the state capital," one of the other children, a little boy, piped up.

Fargo grinned down at him as Hannah's sobs faded away to snuffles. "That's right, son. What's your name?"

"Jonas."

"You ever been to Jefferson City, Jonas?"

"No, sir. I ain't never been nowhere 'cept Braxton's Lick."

"That's the little town close to our farm," Junie explained. Now that Fargo could see her better, he could tell that she was in her late teens, perhaps as old as twenty. Her mouth twisted bitterly as she added, "What used to be our farm."

"Didn't you come through Bear Creek?" asked Fargo.

Junie nodded. "Yes, but it's not much of a town, just a store and a roadhouse and a church."

"How far back up the road is it?"

"About two miles."

Hannah had stopped crying now. In fact, she seemed to have gone to sleep as she leaned against Fargo's chest.

"It must have been pretty late when you came through there," Fargo said. "Why didn't you stop and spend the night?"

"You think folks're gonna take us in outta the goodness of their hearts?" Calvin asked with a bleak laugh. "We got no money. We been spendin' nights in the woods."

"Until this norther blew through today and it started getting cold," Fargo murmured.

Junie nodded.

"Well, you can't stay in the woods tonight," Fargo went on.

"What choice do we have?" Calvin asked.

"Turn around and come on back to Bear Creek with me. We'll stay at that roadhouse tonight and figure out in the morning what you ought to do next."

Junie said, "It won't do any good, Mr. Fargo. We— we stopped and tried to see if the man who runs the roadhouse would give us a little food. He just ran us off. I know he wouldn't let us stay there without paying."

7

"Don't worry about that," Fargo said, thinking about the pouch of double eagles he had in his saddlebags. He had money left over from his last job, and he'd run the total up even more during a poker game in Fort Smith a week earlier. "I can pay for all of us."

"Haddons don't take charity," Calvin said.

Still looking at Junie, Fargo said, "That's your family name? Haddon?"

She nodded. "I'm Junie. I'm the oldest. Calvin comes next, then Luke and Jonas and Sally and Hannah. Arlo's the baby."

"I ain't a baby," Arlo protested. He was about five, Fargo estimated.

"No, you're sure not, son," Fargo told him with a smile. "But I'll bet you're cold and wouldn't mind getting in out of this wind."

"That'd be all right," Arlo said.

"It would be more than all right," Junie said. "It would be a real blessing."

"Let's go then. Tell you what." Fargo set Hannah on the Ovaro's back. "I reckon three or four of you can ride. This horse of mine is pretty strong."

The stallion turned his head and looked back, as if to ask Fargo if he really knew what he was doing. The Ovaro would cooperate, though. He might not like hauling around a passel of young'uns, but he would do it if Fargo wanted him to.

Fargo boosted Sally and Jonas onto the horse, then lifted Arlo and perched him in front of his sisters and brother. That left Junie, Calvin, and Luke to walk, along with Fargo. He grasped the Ovaro's reins and said, "We'd better get moving. It's going to be dark before we get to Bear Creek."

The group started north along the road, but it took only a few steps for Fargo to realize that Calvin wasn't coming with them. He stopped and looked back at the youngster, who was probably sixteen or seventeen.

"You don't listen too good, do you, mister?" Calvin said. "I told you Haddons don't take charity."

"Everybody needs a helping hand now and then. Folks have helped me plenty of times in my life. Don't think of it as charity. Time'll come when you can help out somebody else. Things have a way of evening up."

"Come on, Calvin," Junie urged. "I know you promised Pa you'd take care of us, but Mr. Fargo's right. We can't stay outside tonight."

Calvin crossed his arms over his chest and glared at them stubbornly. Fargo was beginning to wonder if he was going to have to pick him up and carry him, which would probably necessitate tapping him on the jaw and knocking him out first, when Arlo called, "Yeah, come on, Calvin! Don't be a jackass!"

Even under these dire circumstances, Junie had to struggle not to laugh as she said, "Don't talk like that, Arlo. You know Mama wouldn't like it."

"How would I know that?" Arlo asked innocently. "I don't even remember Mama."

Fargo handed the Ovaro's reins to Junie and walked closer to Calvin. "Come on with us," he said. "I'm going to need you to tell me how you folks came to be in this predicament. I know your pa's counting on you to do the best thing for your brothers and sisters."

"Pa ain't countin' on nothin'," Calvin muttered. "He's dead."

Fargo had sort of figured as much. The Haddon youngsters were orphans. He felt a pang of sympathy.

"I reckon we can go back to Bear Creek," Calvin went on. "But I'll figure out a way to pay you for whatever you spend on us. We got to stand on our own feet."

"Fair enough," Fargo said. He wasn't really interested in any repayment. He just wanted Calvin to come on and, like Arlo said, stop being a jackass.

Fargo walked back to the others. Calvin fell in step beside him. Taking the reins from Junie, Fargo headed north, curbing his normal stride a little so that the others could keep up without having to hurry.

Shadows continued to gather, even though Fargo thought it was only a little after four o'clock in the afternoon. At this time of year, with the thick overcast, that was late enough for night to fall. They had gone only about a mile before darkness settled down around them.

But Bear Creek shouldn't be more than another mile ahead of them, Fargo reminded himself, and he could see well enough to keep them on the road.

"Them woods are awful dark," Jonas said from the back of the stallion. "You reckon there's any haints or hobgoblins out there, Mr. Fargo?"

"I doubt it. Even if there is, they won't bother us."

"How do you figure that?"

"Well, it's always seemed to me like the things that lurk in the dark must be as afraid of us as we are of them. Otherwise they wouldn't hide all the time," Fargo said. "You take most folks, even your haints and hobgoblins, and they just want to be left alone to go about their business. You wouldn't sneak up on a ghost and holler boo at him, would you?"

"No, sir," Jonas said fervently.

"Then if you leave him alone, I expect he'll leave you alone."

"That don't make sense," Hannah said. "It's a ghost's job to scare folks."

"How do you know?" Fargo asked. "You ever sit down and talk to one?"

"Lordy, no!"

"Well, then, you don't really know. A ghost might have some other job entirely. Maybe he scares folks sometimes so they'll go away and stop interfering with his real work."

From where he walked alongside Fargo, Junie, and Calvin, Luke Haddon asked, "What sort of work would a ghost have besides scarin' people?"

"I don't know," Fargo said. "But I'm not going to ask one, either. He might up and holler boo at me."

Junie was unable to contain her laughter this time. Except for Calvin, the others joined in. Calvin still trudged along, and even though Fargo couldn't see the youngster's face now, he was willing to bet that there was a surly expression on it.

The talk about ghosts had helped to pass some of the time, and it wasn't long before Fargo spotted a light in front of them, maybe a quarter of a mile away. As they drew closer he could tell that it was the glow from a window, which meant they had to be getting close to Bear Creek.

It was a good thing, too, because drops of cold rain began to fall, spitting down intermittently from the dark heavens. Fargo picked up the pace, not wanting the children to get soaked before they could get in out of the weather.

The rain still wasn't falling hard by the time they reached the tiny crossroads settlement. The church stood on one corner, the store on another, and the sprawling tavern and roadhouse was across the road. The place was built of logs and had a long covered porch on the front of it. A shed and a pole corral stood out back.

"Go up on the porch out of the rain and wait for me," Fargo told the youngsters as he lifted the smaller ones down from the Ovaro's back. "I'll take my horse and put him up, and then we'll go in."

He hated to have them stay outside any longer than necessary, but since they had gotten a hostile reception here earlier, he thought it best to be with them when they went inside.

He unfastened the corral gate and led the stallion inside. Several horses were already huddled together under the shed, which had its north side closed off. At least they were out of the wind. Fargo got the rig off the Ovaro. Then, carrying his saddle on his left shoulder and his Henry rifle in his right hand, he walked around to the front of the roadhouse.

He placed the saddle on the porch and shifted the rifle to his left hand. "Come on," he said to the Haddons as he turned the latch on the door and swung it open.

The air inside the roadhouse was thick with smoke from pipes and oil lamps, but at least it was warm. Flames leaped and crackled in a big stone fireplace on the wall to Fargo's left.

A crudely built bar stood to Fargo's right, and rough-hewn tables, some with chairs and some with benches, were scattered between the bar and the fireplace. A door in the rear wall no doubt led to rooms that travelers could rent for the night.

Three men sat at one of the tables, drinking and playing cards. From the looks of it, they were the only customers. The man behind the bar used a dirty rag to wipe it as he smiled at Fargo. He was short but powerfully built, with a bald head and a bristling black beard shot here and there with gray.

"Howdy, mister," he greeted Fargo in friendly enough fashion, but then his smile disappeared as he looked past the big man in buckskins at the figures filing in behind him. "Hey! I done told you little tramps you ain't welcome here!"

"They're not tramps," Fargo said in a hard-edged voice. "They're children, and they're with me."

The proprietor frowned. "Sorry, mister. I don't mean no offense to you." He gestured at the youngsters. "But they come around here earlier today, beggin', and I had to run 'em off."

"We just wanted a little food," Calvin said. "We don't have much, and we'd have been willin' to work for it."

"Yeah, well," the man blustered, "when I said that sis there could work for whatever y'all wanted, y'all got mad and left. Ain't my fault."

Fargo glanced at Junie. In the light from the oil lamps scattered around the room, he saw that she was blushing from embarrassment. His jaw tightened in anger.

He stalked over to the bar and placed the rifle on it. Then he reached down to his calf and drew the long, heavy-bladed Arkansas toothpick from the fringed sheath that was strapped on his leg. He held up the wicked-looking knife so that the light glittered on its razor-sharp blade.

"You know what this is?" he asked quietly.

The proprietor's eyes widened, and he swallowed hard. "Sure I do. That's an Arkansas toothpick."

Fargo leaned closer to him and said, "That's right. And if you make one more crude comment directed at that young lady—or at any of those children—I'll take this Arkansas toothpick and show you how well it carves up meat."

The proprietor licked lips that had gone dry. "You . . . you can't come in here and threaten me like that," he said. "This is my place."

"I didn't threaten you." Fargo shifted his grip on the knife and suddenly drove its point straight down into the bar. When he let go, it stood up where it was, quivering slightly from the impact. "When I talk about meat, you're drawing your own conclusions."

"I . . . I just don't like beggars."

"Neither do I. But I like heartless bastards even less." Fargo wrapped his fingers around the toothpick's handle and wrenched it free from the bar. He slid it back in its sheath.

"All right," the man said abruptly. "I'll give 'em some food."

"No, you won't. I can pay for it." Fargo took one of the double eagles from his pocket, where he had placed it earlier. He dropped the coin on the bar. "And for rooms where they can spend the night, too."

"Sure, sure." The proprietor didn't make a move yet to scoop the coin off the bar. "I got a couple rooms empty. Reckon that'll be enough?"

Fargo nodded. The girls and the boys could split up, and he could bunk in with Calvin, Luke, Jonas, and Arlo. The boys could have whatever bed there was, and he would make up a pallet on the floor. Fargo had slept in worse circumstances, many a time. At least they'd be in out of the wind and rain.

The rain had picked up, in fact. He heard it rattling on the roof. It was a lonesome sound.

Fargo nodded toward the double eagle that still lay on the bar. "I expect that'll be enough to cover some hot food, too."

"I got a little stew left in the pot, and some biscuits."

Fargo nodded, willing to be friendly now as long as the proprietor kept a civil tongue in his head. "That'll be fine. We're much obliged."

The proprietor finally picked up the coin. "Stew's in the pot in the fireplace. You folks help yourselves. I'll get the biscuits."

14

As the proprietor turned away, the door leading to the rear of the roadhouse opened, and a man came through it, followed by a woman. The man was roughly dressed, and it didn't surprise Fargo when he went over to the table to join the other three.

The woman was around twenty-five, with light brown hair that fell around her shoulders. Her face had started to show some of the lines of hard living, but she retained enough freshness to tell Fargo that she had probably been quite a beauty a few years earlier.

As it was, she was still attractive, with an appealing shape under the simple gray dress she wore. The dress was cut low in front, revealing the swells of her breasts. She had a lace shawl around her shoulders.

The man who had come from the back sat down, and another man stood up. He said something in a low voice to his companions, who laughed. Then he came over to the woman and took hold of her arm, saying, "Come on, honey. It's my turn."

Fargo had figured out as soon as the woman came into the room what her line of work was. It didn't surprise or offend him, but it did sort of bother him that it was going on right here in front of the Haddon youngsters.

He wasn't the guardian of their morals or anything like that, he reminded himself. He intended to see to it that they didn't freeze to death or starve, but other than that it wasn't really any of his business.

Wooden bowls were stacked on the fireplace mantel. Fargo ushered the children in that direction, saying, "Come on, let's get some of that stew. Smells good, doesn't it?"

Behind him, the woman standing beside the bar said to the man who had taken her arm, "Not now, all right? You'll have to wait a while."

The man snorted. "Wait, hell! I ain't got time to wait, and I ain't in the mood to, neither. Get on back there, girl."

Fargo heard the exchange. The man spoke loudly enough so that everybody in the room heard what he said. A glance at Junie showed Fargo that she had her eyes pointed toward the floor. Calvin was looking down, too. The others, except for maybe Luke, were too young to really know what was going on.

He lifted the bowls down from the mantel and started handing them around. "Here you go. Looks like there's some spoons here, too—"

"Let go of me!" the whore said. "Grundy, make him leave me alone. I'm tired."

"Nobody gives a damn if you're tired," the proprietor said. "You got a job to do. You better go do it."

The customer tightened his grip and started to tug on the woman's arm. "Come on."

Suddenly, she let out an angry scream and slapped him across the face as hard as she could. He jerked back, his face reddening where she had struck him.

"You damn slut!" he yelled. He brought up his fist and hit her in the face with it, knocking her against the bar. On the other side of the room, Junie raised her hand to her mouth and muffled a soft cry of horror at the violence. She turned her head to look at Fargo.

"Yeah," he said as he handed her the last of the bowls. "You and Calvin make sure all the kids stay over here."

Then he strode across the room toward the bar, where the man who had been slapped had drawn back his fist to strike another blow. Grundy, the proprietor, looked upset but wasn't making any move to stop him. The man started to swing.

Fargo's hand closed around his wrist, stopping the

blow in midair. The man's head jerked toward him, his mouth contorting in a snarl. "Who the hell—"

Fargo started to squeeze. The man gasped as bones grated together in his wrist. "That's no way to treat a lady, hombre," Fargo said.

The man's other hand plucked a knife from a sheath at his waist. With a curse, he thrust the blade straight at Fargo's belly.

Fargo sucked in his stomach and turned aside so that the knife barely grazed his sheepskin jacket.

At the same time he twisted hard on the man's wrist. A sharp crack sounded as bone broke this time. The man screamed in pain and dropped his knife.

The three men at the table exploded from their chairs. "Get that bastard!" one of them bellowed. They charged at Fargo.

Keeping his grip on the broken wrist and grabbing the man's shirt as well, Fargo swung him around and threw him right into the path of his companions. They couldn't check their rush in time and collided with the man. A couple of them got their legs tangled up and sprawled on the floor, landing on top of the man whose wrist Fargo had broken.

The fourth man managed to stay on his feet, though, and he waded in, swinging roundhouse punches as he tried to trap Fargo against the bar. Fargo ducked under the sweeping blows and drove a fist into the man's midsection. That doubled him over. Fargo put a hand on top of the man's head and pushed. The shove sent him backward, where he tripped over his friends and fell to the puncheon floor beside them.

Fargo was sure the three who weren't injured would pick themselves up and come after him again, so while they were down he drew the heavy, long-barreled Colt from the holster on his right hip and leveled it at them, earing back the hammer as he did so. They stopped struggling to get to their feet as they found themselves staring down the barrel of the gun.

"Now we could waltz around here for a while," Fargo said, "but I'm not in the mood for that. I'm hungry, and I'm just now starting to warm up after being chilled to the bone out there. Seems to me the simplest thing to do would be to shoot the four of you and be done with it."

"For God's sake, mister," Grundy said in a quavering voice. "Don't kill 'em."

"Maybe what they ought to do is get up and get out of here while they still can," Fargo said.

"Yeah." Grundy wiped the back of his hand across his mouth. "Yeah. You boys heard the man. Get on out of here."

"This ain't right," one of them protested. "You broke Luther's arm."

"It was his wrist," Fargo corrected. "And he started it by attacking that woman and then trying to shove a knife in my guts. He's lucky he's not hurt worse than he is."

More grumbling and cursing came from the men, but they got up and helped their injured friend to his feet. The four of them stumbled toward the door. The wind howled as they opened the door and went out into the night. Fargo walked over and slammed the door behind them.

He lowered the Colt but didn't holster it, not trusting that the men wouldn't try to surprise him by busting back in with guns blazing. If they did, he intended to give them a hot lead welcome.

They didn't, and a minute later, he heard horses moving off outside. The men had decided on the better part of valor. Fargo was glad of that. Despite his threats, he didn't really want to kill anybody.

Maybe the Haddon youngsters didn't know that. They were all staring at him like he had grown a second head. He smiled at them, slid his iron back into leather, and said, "Go ahead and fill your bowls while that stew's still warm."

He went to the bar, where the woman stood rubbing her cheek where the man had punched her. She would have a bruise, but maybe it wouldn't be too bad.

"Are you all right?" Fargo asked her.

"Yeah," she said uncertainly. Then her voice grew stronger as she nodded and went on, "I'll be fine. Thanks, mister. I know Luther Copeland. He'd've beaten the hell out of me once he got started."

Fargo looked at Grundy. "That's the kind of customers you let in here?"

"Hey, those boys are good customers," the proprietor said defensively. "They always pay what they owe."

"Are they always so rough with the lady?"

"You can stop calling me a lady, mister," she said. "We all know what I am."

"I wouldn't let anybody hurt Lizbeth," Grundy said.

She gave a humorless laugh. "Oh, no, Grundy would never let anybody hurt me. I'm his cousin, you see, so he feels some family responsibility toward me."

Fargo frowned. "You've got your cousin working the back room of this place?"

Grundy fidgeted with the bar rag and wouldn't meet Fargo's eyes. "It's her choice," he said in a surly voice.

Lizbeth laughed again, and it sounded a little more genuine this time. "He's right. You might as well leave him alone, mister. You can't shame him, and it's too late to make him grow a spine."

"Fine one to talk about shame," Grundy muttered, still without looking up.

Lizbeth shook her head, turned away from him, and put a hand on Fargo's arm. "What's your name?"

"Skye Fargo."

"Skye . . . That's an unusual name. Suits you, though." She lowered her voice and inclined her head toward the youngsters, who were now gathered around the fireplace, eating stew and not looking at the bar. "Is that your brood?"

Fargo smiled and shook his head. "I ran into them on the road a little while ago. They were walking, don't have much food and I suspect no money. I was afraid they might freeze to death if I didn't get them in out of the weather, especially the little ones."

"So you adopted them?"

"Temporarily, I reckon you could say."

"They were here earlier," Grundy put in. "You were asleep then. I ran 'em off."

"I'll bet you offered to help them and let that blond-haired girl pay for it," Lizbeth said scathingly. "She's pretty, and you never minded 'em being young, did you, Grundy? I was fourteen when you cornered me in my folks' barn, as I recall."

"Damn it, Lizbeth—"

"Settle down," she said. "If you're going to act like scum, don't be surprised when somebody points out that you're turning green."

With a shake of his head, Grundy moved off down the bar. "I still got to get those biscuits," he said, as much to himself as to Fargo and Lizbeth.

"Don't mind me, Skye," she said. "I get mean sometimes and start to pick at ol' Grundy. He's not really such a bad sort most of the time, though."

Fargo had his doubts about that, but he didn't want

to talk about Grundy. He said, "I think I'll go get some of that stew while there's still some left."

"Sure, Skye. You do that."

He walked over to the fireplace. The youngsters looked up at him with even wider eyes than before, and he regretted that they'd had to see him fighting and threatening those men with his Colt. They probably thought he was some sort of border ruffian now.

Sure enough, after a minute Jonas worked his courage up and said, "Mr. Fargo, are you an owlhoot?" Junie tried to shush him, but the question was already out.

Fargo smiled and shook his head as he filled a bowl with stew from the pot. "No, I'm not an outlaw, Jonas. I work at a lot of different things, but they're honest jobs like scouting for the army and guiding wagon trains and laying out new routes for stagecoach lines. Sometimes I even work with the law and help track down folks who are missing."

"You said you have a job waiting for you in Jefferson City," Junie said.

Fargo sat down on one of the benches, enjoying the warmth that came from the fire. "That's right. A fellow I know owns a stagecoach line that runs from back east and ends there. He wants to expand on westward, and I'm going to figure out the best route for him and help him get his way stations set up."

"That don't sound very excitin'," Luke said.

"Oh, I'm not looking for excitement," Fargo said. "I'm a peaceable man."

Calvin grunted. "Yeah, you looked real peaceable when you were beatin' those fellas up."

"I didn't start that trouble," Fargo pointed out.

"No, but you pulled your gun on 'em mighty quick." Calvin's voice was harsh. "We've run into a lot of men lately who are quick to use their guns—and hang ropes, too."

Junie caught her breath and glared at her oldest brother. A couple of the younger children started to cry quietly. Obviously, Calvin's words had reminded them of something that saddened them. Fargo suspected it had something to do with how they had become orphans.

He was curious about their story, but he wasn't the sort of man to pry. If any of them wanted to tell him about it, they could do it when they were good and ready.

"I think I'd better get the little ones to bed," Junie said. She stood up and herded Sally, Jonas, Hannah, and Arlo toward the door in the rear of the roadhouse. Lizbeth had already retreated back there.

Grundy came out from behind the bar and stopped Junie, handing her a canvas bag. "Here's those biscuits, in case any of the young'uns get hungry durin' the night. And there's enough there for in the mornin', too."

Junie managed to smile and nod, but she was obviously uncomfortable this close to Grundy. "Thank you."

"And, uh, I'm sorry about what I said earlier. I wasn't thinkin'. I, uh, hope y'all will forgive me."

Grundy glanced at Fargo, who wondered if the apology was meant as much for him as it was for Junie. Clearly, Grundy didn't want to be on Fargo's bad side.

Junie smiled again and took the children on into the back. "Rooms to your left," Grundy called after her.

Fargo said to Calvin and Luke, "You fellas can turn in whenever you want. I'll probably step out to the corral and check on my horse one more time before I go to sleep."

Calvin stared into the flames and without looking at Fargo asked, "Why are you doin' this?"

"Helping you, you mean?"

"Yeah. Nobody does anything to help somebody unless they figure on gettin' something out of it themselves." The boy finally turned his head to stare at Fargo. "You want to bed Junie, too, don't you?"

Fargo set his empty stew bowl aside and met Calvin's gaze squarely. "If you were a few years younger," he said, "I'd turn you over my knee and paddle you for talking like that. If you were older, I'd probably bust you in the mouth. I'm trying to help you because I think it's the right thing to do. That's all."

"Yeah," Calvin said, but he didn't sound convinced.

"Go to bed," Fargo said disgustedly as he stood up. Some folks were just hard to help.

He had unbuttoned his jacket earlier. Now he fastened the buttons again as he went to the door and stepped outside. The cold wind smacked him in the face, and he felt little icy granules. The rain had turned to sleet. He left the shelter of the porch and walked around the building to the shed.

The horses were all right, although the Ovaro tossed his head and let Fargo know in no uncertain terms that he would have preferred being somewhere much warmer, maybe with a nice thick carpet of grass on the ground. Fargo assured him they would get there sooner or later.

The temperature had to be freezing or below, because the sleet was beginning to form little icy patches on the ground. Fargo was walking toward the porch when one of his boots slipped on the ice. He stumbled a little before he caught his balance.

And as he did so, a bullet whispered past his cheek to slam into the thick log wall of the roadhouse.

Even over the howling of the wind, Fargo heard the

crack of the rifle and saw the orange spurt of muzzle flame under the trees to his left. He twisted in that direction and palmed out the Colt as he dropped to one knee. Another rifle roared and sent a slug over his head. Fargo brought up the revolver and fired twice, shifting his aim between the shots. Someone cried out in pain.

A water barrel stood next to the wall. Fargo went to the ground and rolled behind it. A bullet struck the barrel and threw splinters in the air. As he came up in a crouch, Fargo aimed at the muzzle flash and triggered again.

No more shots came from the trees.

Fargo waited patiently behind the barrel. Could be the bushwhackers were waiting for him to move out into the open again. He thought he heard hoofbeats fading into the distance, but with the wind blowing as hard as it was, it was difficult to be sure.

"Hey!" Grundy called from the corner of the porch. "What's goin' on out here?"

"Better stay back, Grundy," Fargo told him. "Somebody just took a few shots at me."

Grundy cursed. "I'll bet it was Sandon, Wilbur, and Lindsey."

"Copeland's friends?"

"Yeah." Disregarding Fargo's advice, Grundy stepped down off the porch and came along the wall of the building, holding a shotgun in his hands. He pointed the greener toward the trees that grew up close to the roadhouse. "I'll cover you. Let's get back inside."

The man's behavior surprised Fargo a little. He said, "I didn't expect you to side with me in this."

"Well, I'll tell you. . . . I'm a pretty sorry son of a bitch, like Lizbeth says. I know it. But I don't like anybody shootin' up the place. It riles me."

Nobody shot anymore as Fargo and Grundy made

their way back inside. Fargo knew he had winged at least one of the bushwhackers. When they had seen that he was going to put up a fight and that they might be the ones who got killed, they'd probably given up on the idea of vengeance and gone off to lick their wounds.

That didn't mean they might not be back. Fargo knew he was going to have to keep his eyes and ears open for trouble as long as he was in this neck of the woods.

The Haddon youngsters had heard the shots, too. They were all in the roadhouse's main room again, crowded close to the door to the rear. As Fargo and Grundy came in, Junie asked anxiously, "Are you all right, Mr. Fargo?"

"I'm fine," he told her. "No need to worry about me."

"We heard shootin' . . ." Calvin began.

Fargo nodded. "Somebody tried to ambush me from the trees. I figure it was those troublemakers I ran off earlier."

"Yeah," Calvin said. "Must've been who it was."

But something about the way he said it, and the furtive glance he exchanged with Junie, made Fargo wonder. It looked and sounded almost like Calvin thought the bushwhackers might have been someone else.

That didn't make any sense—unless . . .

From what Fargo had gleaned so far, the children were running away from some sort of trouble that had taken the life of their father and left them orphaned. Calvin had mentioned guns and hang ropes.

Maybe he thought that whoever had been responsible for the death of their father might come after them, too.

Fargo didn't know about that, but he thought it was a lot more likely the men who had taken those shots at him had been the ones he'd run off earlier. Still, he told himself, it might be a good idea if he tried to get more details from Calvin and Junie in the morning. If he planned to help them get where they were going, he needed to know what he was up against.

It took him a moment to realize that he had decided to continue helping them, rather than going on his way to Jefferson City.

Ed Morrisey, the man who had offered Fargo the job of helping to set up the westward expansion of his stage line, wouldn't be starting the actual operation until spring, and that was more than a month off. Fargo could afford to spend some time giving the youngsters a hand. Morrisey would just have to wait.

"All the excitement's over," Fargo told them. "Better go get some sleep."

The younger ones were reluctant to go to bed, as kids always were for fear they might miss something interesting or exciting, but they were tired, too, and didn't complain too much as they returned to their rooms. Calvin and Junie didn't linger, either.

Grundy set a mug of beer and a shot of whiskey on the bar and said to Fargo, "I figured you might could use these."

Fargo unbuttoned his jacket again, thumbed his hat to the back of his head, and picked up the whiskey. He downed the shot, enjoying the warmth that it kindled in his belly. He washed it down with a sip of the beer.

When Fargo reached for another coin, Grundy shook his head. "No, you paid plenty earlier. Whatever you want tonight, it's covered. In the morning at breakfast, too."

"Generous of you," Fargo said with a nod. "Is this going to cause trouble for you with those fellas?"

"Copeland and his bunch?" Grundy shook his head.

"They may be mad at me right now, but it won't last long. This place may not look like much, but it's the best place to get a drink this side of Braxton's Lick. When those boys get thirsty enough, they'll be back."

"They looked like they've heard the owl hoot in the night a few times."

Grundy shrugged. "I wouldn't know about that. I don't ask 'em where they get their money, and they don't tell me. Everybody's happy that way."

"Except maybe for the folks they steal it from."

"Are you a lawman?" Grundy asked.

Fargo shook his head. "Nope."

"Well, neither am I."

Fargo wasn't going to stand around arguing morality with the man. He drank the rest of the beer and said, "Reckon I'll turn in."

"I will, too, pretty soon. Won't be any more business on a night like this. Anybody with any sense is already in out of the weather somewhere."

Fargo went to the door into the back and stepped through it into a dim hallway lit by a single candle in a wall holder. There were two doors to his left, two to the right. The Haddon youngsters were in the rooms to the left, he recalled, but he wasn't sure which one Calvin and the other boys were using. He frowned, not wanting to walk in on the girls.

He was saved, at least momentarily, from this dilemma. The door on the right, at the far end of the hall, opened and Lizbeth stepped out. She wore a robe, and her hair looked freshly brushed.

"Skye," she said, "I heard the shots, and then I heard you talking about how somebody ambushed you. Are you really all right?"

"I'm fine," Fargo assured her. "A couple of the bullets came close enough for me to hear them, but that's all."

Lizbeth hugged herself and a little shiver went through her. "I hate to think you might have gotten hurt or even killed."

"Why?" Fargo asked. "You never saw me before tonight."

"That doesn't mean I can't tell that you're a good man. You stepped in to help me without hesitating, and you're trying to look after those kids when you just met them, too. That takes a special sort of man."

Fargo shook his head. "Just a man."

"Well, you think whatever you want to think." Lizbeth came toward him. "I know what sort you are, Skye Fargo."

She was close enough to him now that she was able to reach up and put her arms around his neck. Instinctively, Fargo slipped his arms around her waist and pulled her even closer. His mouth came down on hers as she tilted her head back to receive his kiss.

The fact that she sold herself didn't bother him; he had been with whores in the past, although not while they were working. Some of them were damn fine women who had simply come up short of luck in their lives.

But under the circumstances, with those kids so close by and the walls in this place probably paper-thin, he wasn't sure it was a good idea.

He broke the kiss and said in a half-whisper, "You'd better go on back to bed. It's getting late."

"Come with me," Lizbeth urged.

"I thought you were tired."

She laughed softly. "Somehow, all I have to do is look at you, Skye, and I've got all sorts of energy again."

Fargo brushed his lips across her forehead. "I don't know. . . ."

"If you're worried about the young'uns hearing,

don't be. My room's at the end of the hall. And I can be quiet when I need to." She reached down to his groin and caressed his stiffening shaft through his buckskin trousers. "Although from what I feel here, I might want to scream a little."

Fargo chuckled. "You're a brazen woman."

"That's my job."

He tensed. If she just thought of him as a potential customer, then he wanted no part of it.

She must have sensed his reaction, because she said hurriedly, "I didn't mean it like that, Skye. I swear I didn't. I really do want you. Nobody—nobody's been as nice to me in a long time."

Her touch continued to arouse him. Fargo thought she was telling the truth. He was willing to give her the benefit of the doubt, anyway.

"All right," he said. He leaned forward and kissed her again. Her lips parted eagerly under his as his tongue speared between them. Her hand grew more urgent at his groin.

After a moment she pulled her head back and said breathlessly, "Come on. Let's go to my room."

Holding his hand, she led him to the door and inside the small room. Most of the space was taken up by a bed, a wardrobe, a small table with a basin of water and a candle on it, and a single chair.

Lizbeth stood beside the bed as her fingers went to the robe's belt and untied it. She shrugged it off and tossed it over the back of the chair. The room was cool. Not much heat filtered back here from the fireplace in the main room. But despite the chill she stood there nude and let Fargo look at her for a long moment.

Her body was as nice as he thought it would be, with apple-sized breasts that were still firm, a flat belly, and sensuously curving hips. The hair that formed a triangle at the juncture of her thighs was thick and luxuriant and a slightly darker shade than that on her head. Her skin was smooth and creamy.

The brown nipples that crowned her breasts were perfect circles. They puckered, but whether from excitement or the cold, Fargo didn't know. Probably both. He stepped closer to her, filled his hands with the firm globes of female flesh, and used his thumbs to strum the pebbled buds.

Lizbeth closed her eyes for a second and sighed in pleasure at his touch. Fargo's left hand continued toying with her right breast as he put his right hand on her back and slid it down to her rump. His fingers spread as he caressed her plump left cheek.

"Oh, Skye," she murmured as she pushed her pelvis against his groin.

"Better get into bed and get under the covers," he told her. "You're going to get cold."

"No. I'm hot. I'm burning up inside. I don't think I'll ever be cold again."

For a second another doubt flitted across his mind. Her words sounded like typical whore talk, meaningless other than its intention of working up a customer so that he'd finish off quicker.

But she molded her soft nude body against him and reached up to lock her hands together behind his neck. She pulled his head down and kissed him again, and Fargo was convinced that the urgency in her lips was real.

Mentally, he said the hell with it. Even if she was just grateful for his earlier help and was acting, she was damned good at it.

She gasped and started tugging at his clothes. He helped her, and within moments he was nude, too.

The long, thick pole of male flesh jutted out proudly from his groin. Lizbeth wrapped her hands around it and whispered eagerly, "Oh, my God! Skye!"

"Remember what you said about being quiet," he reminded her with a smile.

She sat down on the edge of the bed, still holding on to him with both hands. "You'd better give me something to occupy my mouth, then."

She leaned forward. Her pink tongue darted out. The tip of it circled the head of his shaft. The light, teasing oral caress made his member throb, and that pulse went all the way through him.

Lizbeth kept up the exquisite torment for several minutes, licking and kissing and squeezing. When at last she opened her mouth and took him inside, he almost exploded then and there. It took a supreme effort of will to keep from doing so. Lizbeth steadied the shaft with one hand and drew it deeper into her mouth, while the other hand strayed down to cup the heavy sacs beneath.

Fargo rested his hands on her head and pumped his member in and out between her lips. Sensations cascaded through him. He was at a fever pitch and had to continue fighting off the urge to lose control.

Finally Lizbeth lifted her head and gasped for breath as she threw back the thick comforter and blankets on the bed. Lying down, she spread her thighs in wanton invitation. The candlelight sparkled on the dew that beaded the hair around the opening of her sex.

"Take me now, Skye!" she begged. "Please!"

Fargo didn't need any more urging. He moved between her legs and positioned the head of his shaft against her. A thrust of his hips sheathed it inside her. She cried out softly as he penetrated her.

Fargo kissed her again to keep her quiet as he drove his member in and out of her in a steady rhythm. It was a timeless, universal cadence, and it quickly lifted both of them to new heights of arousal. Lizbeth's inner muscles clasped him in their heated grip as Fargo withdrew partially and then plunged deep inside her again. She panted into his open mouth.

Lizbeth had been right—it was no longer cold in the room. It was hot, in fact, a blazing desert heat such as Fargo had encountered in Death Valley or the *Jornada del Muerto*—the Journey of Death—in New Mexico Territory.

Appropriate names, for was not the culmination of such passionate coupling sometimes known as the Little Death?

That thought passed fleetingly through Fargo's mind and then was gone, washed away by the flood of sensation sweeping through him. He lunged into Lizbeth a final time and unleashed his climax. She spasmed underneath him and probably would have screamed if he hadn't been kissing her so hard.

Then they both relaxed as they coasted down the far side of the peak. With his manhood still buried inside her, Fargo cradled her in his arms. In a few minutes, as the heat of their lovemaking faded and the chill of the room returned, he pulled the covers over them, creating a cocoon of warmth.

Lizbeth began to nuzzle his shoulder, nipping with her teeth and sucking with her lips. Fargo stroked her hair. She whispered, "Thank you, Skye. I—I had almost forgotten what the real thing felt like."

Again Fargo felt a twinge of doubt, followed immediately by one of guilt for doubting her. It was true that Grundy had said he'd already paid enough to cover anything he wanted tonight, but he didn't believe that Lizbeth fell into that category. He knew the truth when he heard it.

He propped himself on an elbow and said, "It was

33

mighty nice, all right. Nice enough I wish I could spend the night right here and maybe do it again."

Lizbeth moved her hips provocatively. "Why can't you?"

"It wouldn't be right for those kids to see me coming out of your room in the morning. I haven't been around youngsters all that much, but I've heard they're usually early risers."

"You don't want to slip into their room and wake them up, though."

That brought him back to his earlier problem of not knowing which room the girls were in. As the solution occurred to him, he said, "I think I'll go back out in the main room and bed down on one of those benches. I've slept in worse places."

"You're going to sleep on an ol' hard bench when you could stay right here in this soft, warm bed?"

Fargo chuckled. "It sounds pretty stupid when you put it like that, but I reckon it's the right thing to do."

With a sigh, Lizbeth shook her head. "If I didn't feel so good right now, I'd be mighty disappointed. To tell the truth, though, I'm not sure I could stand being much happier. I already feel a little like I'm going to bust."

"Glad to be of help," Fargo said with a grin.

She laughed and punched him lightly on the shoulder. "Well, go on if you're going. Don't stay here and torment me if you're not going to do anything about it."

"Yes, ma'am."

Fargo slipped out of bed and shivered as his bare feet touched the cold floor. Quickly, he drew his clothes and boots on. Lizbeth watched him with the covers pulled up tight around her neck.

When he was dressed, he leaned over the bed and gave her another kiss. Then he blew out the candle on the table and slipped out the door, easing it shut behind him.

The door between the rear hall and the main room was open so that some light and heat from the fireplace came through. All the lamps were out, though, Fargo saw as he stepped into the main room. Grundy had gone on to bed. Fargo didn't waste time wondering—or caring—if the man had heard what went on in Lizbeth's room.

Fargo folded up his jacket and used it as a pillow as he stretched out on one of the benches in front of the fire, which had burned low and would soon be nothing but embers. The day had been a long one, and he was tired. He didn't think it would take him long to go to sleep.

But as he was dozing off, one of the split-log beams that formed the puncheon floor made a little noise as it shifted. Fargo tensed, knowing what that meant.

Someone was trying to sneak up on him.

3

Several thoughts flashed through Fargo's mind at that instant.

The first was that one of the men who had bush-whacked him earlier had snuck into the roadhouse somehow to lurk in the shadows and wait for another opportunity for vengeance.

The next thought was that Grundy wasn't as trust-worthy as he had tried to appear. Fargo had heard of tavern keepers who murdered their guests during the night, robbing them and disposing of their bodies in some gruesome manner.

And finally he thought that maybe Lizbeth had fol-lowed him out here and wanted to get in some more lovemaking in front of the fireplace. That was the most attractive option, of course.

But the other two alternatives were deadly, and Fargo couldn't afford to discount them. Instinct sent him rolling off the bench to land in a crouch on one knee. At the same time, his hand flashed to his hip and his Colt seemed to leap out of its holster by magic.

The blanket-wrapped figure in front of him stepped back with a soft, startled cry.

Fargo saw instantly that all three of his guesses had been wrong. Blond hair fell around the shoulders of the person who had slipped into the room, and the wide eyes looking at him were blue.

"Junie," Fargo said, "what are you doing out here?"

Her mouth opened but she didn't say anything. After a second, Fargo realized she was staring at the gun in his hand. The barrel was still pointed at her. He lowered it and slipped it back into the holster as he came to his feet.

"Sorry. Didn't mean to scare you."

Junie finally found her voice. "That—that's all right. It's me who ought to apologize, Mr. Fargo. I never should have snuck up on you that way."

"It's all right," Fargo told her. "Probably be a good idea not to do it again, though."

"Don't worry. I won't."

Fargo sat down on the bench and patted it beside him. "Have a seat. You still haven't told me why you're out here."

Carefully, Junie sat down beside him. Even though the firelight was dim, this was the best look Fargo had gotten at her so far. Without the heavy coat and the scarf that had been wrapped around her head, he could see how pretty she was.

"I wanted to talk to you," she said. "I heard somebody in the hall and peeked out the door, and I saw you come in here." She paused. "I thought you were going to stay with Calvin and the boys."

"I realized I didn't know which room they were in, and I didn't want to disturb you young ladies."

She lifted her head a little. "I'm not all that young. I'm nineteen. My ma was married and had two or three young'uns by the time she was my age." With a sigh, she added, "Folks up around home considered me an old maid."

"There are fools everywhere," Fargo pointed out.

"A girl as pretty as you isn't likely to wind up an old maid."

Junie looked down at the floor. In the reddish glow from the dying flames in the fireplace, it was hard to be sure, but Fargo thought she was blushing again.

"If I said I wasn't all that pretty, you'd think I was just fishing for a compliment. And I reckon I would be."

Fargo thought it might be wise to change the subject. "You said you wanted to talk to me. What about?"

"I want to thank you—" she began.

"No need for that," Fargo said with a shake of his head. "I just did what anybody would do who found a bunch of children out in the cold."

"No, that's not true," Junie said firmly. "A lot of folks wouldn't care, and some would try to take advantage, like that Mr. Grundy did."

"Well, I just did what I thought needed to be done. Nothing special about that."

"The only reason you feel that way is because you're a good, honest man."

Fargo laughed. "I'm not so sure how good I am. You might get an argument about that from some folks, like that fella Copeland."

"He got what was coming to him." Junie took a deep breath. "And I think you should get what's coming to you, Mr. Fargo."

She stood up and let the blanket slip off her shoulders. It fell around her feet. Fargo caught his breath as he saw that she was nude underneath it.

In the full bloom of her young womanhood, Junie was breathtakingly lovely. She inhaled deeply again, lifting the full, firm breasts with their large pink nipples. Her skin was fair and covered with hair so pale and fine it was invisible except where the glow from the fire highlighted it. The curves of her body were perfect.

"Junie," Fargo said, and his voice sounded strained to his ears. "Junie, you'd better wrap that blanket around yourself again."

Her lower lip began to tremble. "You—you don't want me, Mr. Fargo?"

That wasn't the problem. Despite the fact that he had been with Lizbeth only a short time earlier, Junie's loveliness had struck Fargo like a fist in the face. She had the sort of earthy power that only one woman in a hundred possessed, and yet there was an innocence about her that made her even more appealing. It was all Fargo could do not to pull her into his arms and feast on everything she was offering him.

But the offer was made out of gratitude, and perhaps fear that he wouldn't continue to help her and her brothers and sisters if she didn't give herself to him. Fargo had never forced a woman in his life, nor taken advantage of one in such an obviously fragile emotional state.

If he did that, he'd be just as big a polecat as Grundy had tried to be.

He didn't argue with her. He picked up the blanket from the floor, stood up, and wrapped it around her. It was a little easier for him to think—not to mention breathe—once all that soft, sleek female skin was covered up.

"It's not that I don't want you, Junie," he said. He hoped that she believed him, because it was certainly the truth. "You're about the prettiest girl I've seen in a month of Sundays. But you shouldn't be doing this with somebody you just met, somebody you don't really know."

Junie inclined her blond head toward the back of the roadhouse. "You went with *her*, didn't you? I saw you with her in the hall. And you just met her and don't really know her."

So she had been spying on him and Lizbeth when they met in the hall. Junie had been busy this evening.

But Fargo couldn't bring himself to be angry with her. He said, "You thought because of that you ought to try the same thing?"

"I thought you might—I thought maybe all you cared about . . ." She couldn't go on. Tears shone in her eyes.

Fargo sat down on the bench and drew her down beside him, making sure that the blanket stayed tight around her. He slipped an arm around her. She leaned her head on his shoulder. He was aware of the potent appeal she still held, but he pushed those thoughts to the back of his mind.

"I helped you and the others because it was the right thing to do," he said, aware that he was echoing what he had told Lizbeth earlier. "You don't owe me anything except maybe some thanks, and you've already said that."

"Mr. Fargo," Junie said between sniffles, "you're—you're just about the kindest man I've ever met."

"I reckon you ought to call me Skye."

"Really? That would be nice."

"Really," Fargo said.

Junie snuggled closer against him. The passionate feelings she had aroused in him gradually faded, to be replaced by more companionable ones.

Even though they both needed sleep, it occurred to Fargo that this might be a good chance to get some of the information he needed if he was going to help them. He said, "Just sitting here with you is mighty nice, Junie, but we need to talk."

She lifted her head and looked at him. "Talk about what?"

"The trouble that you and Calvin and the others are in."

He felt her stiffen against him. "You don't want to hear about all that," she said.

"Actually, I do. I want to help you, and I can't do it if I don't know what the problem is."

"The problem is, we lost our farm and don't have any place to live. That's why we're on our way to Springfield. Like Calvin told you, we've got kinfolks there."

"How did you lose the farm?" Fargo asked.

Junie shook her head. "It's a long story."

"I've got nothing but time," Fargo told her. He nodded toward the glowing embers and the tiny, dancing flames. "And what better place to tell a story than in front of a fire like this, on a cold and rainy night?"

"You're *sure* you want to hear about it?"

"I'm sure," Fargo said.

Junie hesitated a moment longer, but then nodded. "I reckon you've got a right to know, considering everything you've done for us already, Skye. It was like this . . ."

Nobody around that part of the Ozarks knew how long the Braxtons had hated the Haddons, and vice versa. Even the members of the two families weren't sure about the origin of the hostilities.

All they knew was that they hated each other and had been killing each other for such a long time that the hatred between them had grown to be like a living thing, feeding and growing stronger on the very mountain air itself.

Blood had been spilled, and the only answer was more blood.

Black Hugo Braxton had gotten his name from the bushy jet-black beard that came far down over his chest. As a young man some forty years earlier, he had been the worst of the Braxtons, who were the wealthiest, most powerful family around the settlement that bore their name. The salt deposit they claimed had made them rich. Hugo was accustomed to taking whatever he wanted, whether it was a piece of property, another man's horse—or another man's woman.

Hugo was also thought to have murdered at least half a dozen of the Haddon men, but nobody could ever prove it. By nature the Haddons were farmers, peaceful folks who wanted only to be left alone. But they would fight when riled, and they fought against Black Hugo and the rest of the Braxtons. Rifles spoke from ambush in the deep woods; pistols barked as men faced each other in the settlement's lone street; knives glittered in the lantern light and then grew red with gore as they cut and slashed.

People called it a feud, but it was really a war. A war to the death . . .

But then, against all odds, Black Hugo Braxton began to grow old. He still drank the whiskey that he brewed himself, but he wasn't as interested in women or killing Haddons as he used to be. A man who had lived the life Black Hugo had should have been dead ten times over by now. Instead the beard that had given him his name gradually turned white, along with his hair, until he looked more like an Old Testament prophet than he did a hell-raising mountaineer.

Walter Haddon was the last of his family in the area, other than his children. His father, his uncles, his brothers, and his cousins had all lost their lives to the feud, and the womenfolk and young'uns they had left behind had all gone elsewhere to live, away from the mountains.

Walter, though, clung stubbornly to the Haddon

land. There was too much of it for him to work, even with help from his boys Calvin and Luke, so he allowed other families to move onto part of it and work the land on shares. Most of it was bottomland, along the creeks that ran between the steep-sided, pine-covered slopes, and those who knew dirt said the Haddon place had some of the best farmland in the Ozarks on it.

For several years, a sort of unofficial truce held between the Braxtons and the Haddons. Walter and his friends didn't go looking for trouble, and Black Hugo kept a tight rein on his hot-blooded sons, Garrett and Joel.

The Braxton boys would have continued the feud if it was up to them. After hearing all the stories, they thought it was unfair that they had never gotten to kill a bunch of Haddon men and drag some Haddon girls into the bushes to have fun with them the way their pa had done.

But they knew it wouldn't be smart to go against Black Hugo's wishes, even though he was now an old man, so they contented themselves with mischief like shooting a Haddon cow every now and then, or burning a field or a barn. It was better than nothing.

Then, after that period of relative peace, Black Hugo Braxton had, for some unknown reason, looked upon the Haddon bottomland and decided that he wanted it. It was going to be his, no matter what it took to get it.

Give him credit—more than he deserved, probably—but to the surprise of many, Hugo tried the legal approach first. He came to see Walter Haddon and offered to buy him out. The whole place, the bad, nearly useless land along with the good, and for a fair price, too.

But Walter wouldn't sell. That land had been in the

Haddon family for generations. Haddons had come through the Cumberland Gap, along the Wilderness Road, and on to Missouri, and when they reached the Ozarks, they knew they were home. Here they had come and here they would stay, and Walter was nothing if not a Haddon, with a Haddon's stubbornness.

Politely, he had told Hugo that the land wasn't for sale. Not so politely, when his visitor had pressed him about it, Walter had told Black Hugo to go to hell. The shotgun in Walter's hands had emphasized the point.

Hugo had come over in a buggy. He slapped the reins against the backs of the horses, pulled the buggy around, and said angrily, "You ain't heard the last o' this, Haddon!"

"Probably not," Walter shouted back at him, "but the next time we talk it'll be with guns!"

Walter knew it wasn't wise to defy Black Hugo like that. Sometimes, though, a man had no choice.

But it worried him how the clash would affect his children. Mostly they were still too young to be involved in any sort of trouble, but Calvin was seventeen, a prime age for stepping into things he shouldn't. Over Walter's objections, Calvin took to carrying a gun, an old flintlock pistol he had bought with money he earned himself.

Calvin talked a lot, too, about what he would do to Garrett and Joel Braxton if they ever bothered him or any of his family. Garrett and Joel were both older than Calvin, in their early twenties, and already had reputations for drinking and whoring and fighting.

Walter knew that either of them would kill Calvin without even blinking, so he kept the boy as close to home as he could.

The campaign of harassment against Walter and the sharecroppers intensified. Three other families lived on Haddon land, and the heads of those three house-holds came to Walter and told him that something had to be done. Their mules and milk cows had been killed, horses had stampeded through their vegetable gardens, and their crops had gone up in flames. They were ready to quit.

"We've got to be strong," Walter had told them. "Braxton's trying to run us off, but sooner or later he has to see that he's not going to be able to do it. Then he'll leave us alone again."

"I dunno, Walt," lanky, overalled Bill Donner had said. "He seems mighty stubborn to me."

The other two croppers had agreed with Donner. But Walter had persuaded them to hang on and try to wait out Braxton. They agreed—but each of them sent his family away to stay with relatives.

Walter might have done the same thing if he'd had that choice, but his closest kin was in Springfield. That was a long way off, a hundred miles or more. He would have to keep an eye on his children and hope for the best.

He thought about going to the sheriff and asking for help, but it didn't take him long to decide that that wouldn't do any good. Sheriff Oliver Reynolds was married to Hugo Braxton's niece. He wouldn't do anything to oppose Black Hugo.

Perhaps naïvely, though, Walter thought that Reynolds would stay out of the dispute, at least. He wasn't prepared for what happened on that cold winter evening when a lot of hoofbeats sounded outside the house as the family was sitting down to supper.

"Riders comin'," Luke said. He jumped up from the table and went into the front room to look out the window, ignoring his father's warning to be careful. He called back excitedly, "There's a dozen men or more out there, Pa!"

Junie heard her father curse under his breath as he scraped his chair back and stood up. That told her how upset he was. Walter Haddon was a God-fearing man who read the Bible every night. He wouldn't cuss in front of his children unless he was really mad.

Or really scared.

These days Walter kept his shotgun within easy reach. He picked it up from the floor beside his chair and said, "Luke, get back in here!" To his other children, he added, "The rest of you stay here."

Calvin was on his feet. "I'm goin' with you, Pa."

"No, you're not!" Walter made a curt gesture with his free hand. "Sit back down and don't get out of that chair again!"

Walter was a soft-spoken man most of the time, especially with his kids. The younger ones had never heard him sound like this. They stared at him, more than a little frightened themselves.

Carrying the shotgun, Walter stalked into the foyer while Luke came back into the dining room. "What's Pa gonna do?" Luke asked worriedly.

"I don't know," Calvin said, "but I'm not gonna stay here." He started to get up again.

Junie reached over and took hold of his arm. "Pa told you not to interfere."

"I'm not interferin'," Calvin protested. "I just want to help." He tried to pull free, but Junie was older and a little bigger. She kept a tight grip on his arm.

"You can help him by not giving him something else to worry about," Junie said firmly.

Calvin looked like he couldn't decide whether to cuss or cry. He stopped trying to get away from Junie, though, and that was the most important thing at the moment.

Junie heard the front door open, heard her father

step out onto the porch. "Evenin'," Walter said. "What can I do for you boys? Is that you, Sheriff?"

The hard tones of Oliver Reynolds came back. "You're under arrest, Haddon."

"Arrest! What for? I haven't done anything!"

"Hugo Braxton's sworn out a warrant on you. Says you stole three of his cows."

"Braxton!" Walter said the name as if it tasted like the bitterest bile in his mouth. "He's lying. I never stole anything from him."

"That ain't the way we heard it," Reynolds said. His voice dropped, as if he had turned his head to speak to someone else. "Bring Donner up here."

"Donner!" Walter exclaimed. "Bill Donner, is that you? What are you doin' with these men?"

Junie's hands clenched into fists on the dining room table as she heard the cropper's whining tones. "I'm sorry, Walt, but Sheriff Reynolds is the law. I had to tell him the truth about you stealin' those cows from Braxton. I had to tell him I seen the cows in your barn."

"You're a damned liar! Braxton's paid you off, hasn't he? Either that, or you're such a spineless skunk you're tryin' to get on his good side!"

Sheriff Reynolds ordered, "Search the barn."

"Take one step toward that barn and I'll blow your head off!"

Calvin lunged out of his chair, and there was no holding him back this time. He ran out of the dining room, through the foyer, and onto the front porch. Luke was right behind him, and so was Junie. She tried to keep the younger children back, though.

"Pa!" Calvin cried as he stepped onto the porch.

Walter whipped a glance over his shoulder at his eldest son. Junie would never forget the way her father's face looked at that moment: furious about the false charge leveled at him, of course, and proud so that he had to defend his honor and his place, but he was scared, too, and his eyes were haunted, as if he already sensed the futility of what he was doing.

Struggle as a man might, the world sometimes reared up and crushed him, and there wasn't a blessed thing he could do about it. Fair or unfair, there just wasn't a thing he could do.

"Get back in the house!" Walter Haddon hissed at his children. He might not be able to stop the fate barreling down on him, but at least he could try to shield his young'uns from it.

"No, Pa!" Calvin said. He reached for the butt of the pistol tucked behind his belt.

Walter's right arm came around in a backhanded blow that landed squarely on Calvin's jaw. The boy wasn't expecting it. He flew backward like a puppet on a jerked string, and the only reason he didn't fall was because Junie and Luke caught him.

"Take him inside," Walter ordered, his voice breaking a little from the strain. "All of you get inside."

"Come on," Junie said, knowing that they had to do as he asked. She and Luke began to drag the stunned Calvin through the door. With her free hand, she shooed the younger children back toward the dining room. They could still hear everything that went on through the open door, however, and see a little slice of it as well.

In the few moments she had been outside, she had gotten a good look at the group of men on horseback, recognizing not only Sheriff Reynolds and Bill Donner, but also Garrett and Joel Braxton.

The two of them had leered at her, as they always did whenever they caught sight of her in the settlement or on the road. More than once, they had sidled up to her in town and in voices too low for anyone else to hear had told her in filthy terms everything they wanted to do to her, everything they *would* do to her if they ever got the chance.

She hated Garrett and Joel and feared them, too. Suddenly, she wondered if *they* were behind this.

The other men were a couple of Sheriff Reynolds' deputies, along with several cronies of Garrett and Joel Braxton. They weren't alone, either. Junie heard her father say, "Esau? Pete? Is that you? Damn it, Sheriff. Why are they tied up?"

Esau Tompkins and Pete Curry were the other two sharecroppers who worked the Haddon place along with Bill Donner. Junie didn't think they would turn on her father—but she wouldn't have thought that Donner would, either.

"I have warrants for them, too," Reynolds said. "They're part of this. They've been stealin' from Mr. Braxton just like you have, Haddon."

"More damned lies! Bill, tell the sheriff the truth," Walter pleaded.

"Sorry, Walt," Donner said stubbornly. "I've done told him what I know."

"Sheriff!" That was one of the deputies. "Sheriff, here's them cows, like Donner said!"

Junie knew that when her father had turned away to deal with Calvin and get him and the other children back in the house, the deputies must have slipped into the barn to search it as Sheriff Reynolds had ordered. They had found Braxton's cows in there.

But those cows had been put in the barn by somebody else, probably Garrett and Joel and their friends. That was the only explanation that made any sense. Junie knew her father wasn't a thief.

For the first time, Garrett spoke up. He was a tall, handsome young man with the same jet-black hair his father had had as a youngster. Garrett also had a handlebar mustache he kept waxed and twirled. He dressed well and was as vain as a peacock.

He said, "There's your proof, Sheriff. Do your duty and arrest Haddon."

"I've already told him he's under arrest," Reynolds snapped. "Haddon, put that shotgun down and come along peacefully. Nobody will get hurt."

"I'm not going anywhere with you," Walter said defiantly. "I'm not going to let you and the Braxtons railroad me!"

"Hear that, Sheriff?" Joel Braxton said. A year younger than his brother Garrett, he was much slighter in build, with sandy hair and a face like a hatchet. "He's resistin' arrest. You got every right to shoot him down like a dog."

"There's not gonna be any shooting—" Reynolds began.

"Look out!" Garrett yelled. "He's gonna use that shotgun!"

Junie could see her father standing on the porch. True, Walter Haddon held the shotgun in his hands, but it wasn't pointed at anybody. In fact, the double barrels were angled down, toward the porch.

That didn't stop Garrett Braxton. A gun roared, and Walter was driven back as the bullet struck him in the shoulder. Junie's eyes widened in horror as she saw blood splash from the wound. The crimson droplets seemed to hang in the air and take forever to splatter to the porch.

Walter was thrown backward by the impact. He dropped the shotgun. It went off when it hit the porch, but the buckshot didn't do anything except gouge a big hole out of a couple of the boards.

"Grab him!" Joel Braxton cried. "He tried to shoot the sheriff! String him up!"

Yells sounded and bootheels rang on the porch as

men closed in around Walter. Junie ran to the door and screamed, "No!" but they didn't pay any attention to her. She saw that the men who had hold of her father were Garrett, Joel, and their friends. They hustled him down off the porch while Reynolds and his two deputies looked on helplessly, unable—or unwilling—to interfere.

"No need to waste a jail cell or any county money on a trial, Sheriff," Garrett said. "Haddon's a thief, and we all saw him try to murder you just now. We'll take care of him. Come on, boys!"

They started to drag Walter toward the big cottonwood tree beside the barn.

"Damn it, Garrett—" Reynolds called out.

Garrett looked back at the lawman, his face flinty. "I said we'd handle it, Sheriff." The threat in his voice was unmistakable.

Reynolds looked pale and shaken, but after a moment he nodded. This was out of his hands now, he seemed to be saying.

"Bring them other two!" Joel called as he pointed at Tompkins and Curry. "We'll make a party of it!"

"And Donner, too," Garrett added. "He tried to lie his way out of it, but he's just as guilty as the others!"

"No!" Donner shouted in alarm. "I helped you, Garrett! You can't—"

One of the men who was still mounted pulled his horse over next to Donner's and slammed a pistol butt against the cropper's head. Donner pitched limply out of the saddle. A couple of the Braxton men grabbed him and dragged his unconscious form toward the tree. Tompkins and Curry had already been taken there, struggling but unable to escape from the men who had hold of them.

"Good thing we got four ropes!" Garrett said with a laugh.

Junie was so overcome with shock and horror and disbelief that she couldn't do anything except stand there in the doorway and peer out. She wasn't even aware of the children crowding around her, looking on as the awful scene unfolded before them.

Ropes were tossed over a sturdy branch of the cottonwood tree. Donner went up first, since he was out cold and couldn't fight back. One of the ropes was knotted around his neck, and then he was pulled up. Unconscious or not, his instincts took over and made him start kicking as his feet dangled in the air.

Tompkins was next, while Donner was still kicking and swaying back and forth. He managed to get one terrified shriek out before the rope drew tight around his neck and he was hauled off the ground, too. He kicked even harder than Donner.

Fear gave Pete Curry an insane strength. He broke away from the men who held him and tried to run. He had gone only a couple of steps, though, when a gun leaped into Garrett Braxton's hand and blasted. The bullet struck Curry in the back and drove him to the ground, facedown.

Garrett looked over at Reynolds and drawled, "You saw it, Sheriff. Prisoner tried to escape. Good thing you swore us all in as special deputies, so I could shoot him all legal-like."

When Junie's stunned brain recovered enough later for her to think about what had happened, she knew that Garrett and the others hadn't been sworn in as deputies. That was just his way of excusing murder.

But the gray-faced Sheriff Reynolds nodded grimly and went along with the lie. Things had gone too far for him to do anything else.

With a cackle of laughter, Joel Braxton said, "Let's string him up anyway. Nobody'll ever know whether he got shot or hanged first."

Curry's body was pulled up to dangle next to those of Donner and Tompkins. Both of them had stopped kicking by now. That left only Walter Haddon.

"Your turn now, old man," Garrett said to Walter with an ugly grin on his face. "This is what you get for stealing from the Braxtons."

Walter was pale from the loss of the blood that had leaked from his smashed shoulder and soaked his right sleeve. He had enough strength left, though, to say, "Damn you, Garrett. You'll burn in hell for this, and so will your brother and your friends."

Joel cackled again. "We're doin' the Lord's work! Haddons got no place on this earth!"

"Get that rope on him, boys," Garrett ordered coldly.

Junie had to look away. She became aware that the younger children were all sobbing and wailing, and she knew they shouldn't see this. They had seen too much horror already.

Suddenly, Calvin tried to push past her onto the porch. He had regained his senses after being stunned by his father's backhanded blow. Junie grabbed him desperately and hung on for dear life. She thought she and the younger children wouldn't be harmed, but Calvin was old enough the Braxtons might decide to hang him, too, if he tried to interfere.

"Help me, Luke," she cried out. "Hang on to him!"

Together, she and Luke were able to keep Calvin in the house. Out by the barn, Walter Haddon was hauled up at the end of a rope. He kicked a few times, and it was over.

Garrett jerked a thumb at the barn and said, "Burn it down."

Joel hurried into the barn, and when he came out a few minutes later, the glare of flames followed him. Smoke began to billow from the open doors. When the walls caught on fire, the hellish glare illuminated the four figures hanging from the limb of the cotton-wood tree next to the barn.

The Braxton brothers and their friends started toward the house. Sheriff Reynolds and his deputies moved their horses so that they blocked the gang of killers. Reynolds said, "I don't know what you got in mind, Garrett, but you're not gonna harm those kids. There's got to be a line somewhere. There's got to be an end to it."

For a second, Junie thought Garrett was going to draw his gun again and blow Reynolds out of the saddle. But then Garrett smiled and said, "Sure, Sheriff. We wouldn't do anything to hurt kids." His voice hardened as he went on, "But they got to get out of here. With Haddon dead, the county'll be sellin' this place for the taxes. I can tell you right now, my pa will be the only one putting in a bid."

Even in her stunned grief, Junie saw the reason for what had happened. It was all because of the land. The Braxtons had put those cows in the barn and then sworn out a false warrant to give them an excuse to stage this lynching. Everybody in the county knew that Hugo Braxton had his eye on the Haddon place. No one would dare to bid against him when it was put up for auction.

So Black Hugo would get what he wanted—again. And all it had taken was four murders. . . .

Reynolds turned his horse so that he faced Junie, Calvin, and Luke, with the other children crowded in behind them in the doorway. "You youngsters better get out of here first thing in the morning," he told them in a low voice. "I'll leave some men out here tonight to keep an eye on you, but after that . . . Well, it'll be better if you're gone."

Junie struggled to find her voice. "But, Sheriff . . . this isn't right. . . . This is our place—"

"What's right's got nothin' to do with it," Reynolds said in a harsh whisper as he leaned forward in the saddle. Behind him, the roof of the barn blazed up. The flames crackled and roared.

Junie knew the sheriff was right. If they stayed here, sooner or later the Braxtons would come after them, too. They had to leave. They had to let Garrett and Joel and their old bastard of a father win.

"We'll go," she heard herself saying.

"You can't take nothing with you," Garrett called past the sheriff. "Everything on this place belongs to the county now. Clothes on your back and a little food, that's all."

Junie looked imploringly at Reynolds. "Sheriff . . ."

Reynolds looked away and wiped the back of his hand across his mouth. "Legally, Garrett's right. You might not have known this, Miss Junie, but your pa was in arrears to the county already. I got the authority to seize the place and everything on it."

That was why they had waited until now to act, Junie thought. She hadn't known that her father was behind on the taxes, but it didn't surprise her. The Braxtons had made everything so hard that the farm hadn't been as productive as usual lately.

So the Braxtons had seized the opportunity to make murder and a land grab look legal. It was just a facade, of course, but nobody would challenge it. Nobody would defy Black Hugo and his sons.

"We'll go," she said again. "We'll be gone, first thing in the morning."

Reynolds nodded. "That'd be best."

Garrett, Joel, and their friends mounted up then and rode away, laughing. Reynolds shook his head and slowly followed them, leaving the two nervous-looking deputies behind to watch over the place until morning.

Junie tried to wipe away the tears on her face, but they were replaced by new ones as soon as she did. A chilly wind sprang up and made the huge flames dance merrily as they consumed the barn. The heat from the conflagration was enough to char the bodies of the men hanging nearby. The awful scent drifted over to the house and made Junie sick.

She looked up at the heavens over the Ozarks, but there were no answers there—only sparks that rose from the burning barn, glowing brightly as they ascended and then winking out, like new stars being born and dying even as she watched.

4

Fargo couldn't remember the last time he had been filled with such a deep, soul-sickened anger. He had listened quietly as Junic told the story in hushed words. Her voice had trembled a time or two, but for the most part it was steady. Her eyes were still haunted with grief.

"How long ago did this happen?" Fargo asked when Junie finally fell silent.

"A little over a week. It's taken us that long to walk this far from the farm. The little ones can't move very fast."

No, Fargo supposed that they couldn't. They were too young to have been thrown out of house and home after watching their father and his friends being lynched.

He stood up. Mechanically, his hand went to the Colt and drew it from the holster. Standing in front of the dying fire, he opened the revolver's cylinder and checked its chambers. He had replaced the rounds he had fired earlier, so the Colt carried five bullets, with one chamber empty so that the hammer could rest on it. Fargo closed the cylinder and slid the gun back into the holster.

He hadn't really seen the weapon in his hands, even though he seemed to be staring down at it. Instead, his senses had been filled with the picture Junie had so vividly described. He could see the flames leaping from the barn, feel their heat on his face, smell the unholy stench of the hanged men slowly roasting . . .

"Skye . . . ?" Junie asked in a half whisper. "Skye, you look so . . . so . . ."

Fargo's nostrils flared as he dragged a deep breath into his body. His face cleared as he tamped down the outrage inside him. He knew what had to be done. It wasn't what he *wanted* to do next—that would have involved riding up to Braxton's Lick and spreading a little blood and flame and destruction himself—but it was necessary.

He sat down again and managed to put a faint smile on his face as he turned to Junie and said, "All right, here's what we're going to do. You and your brothers and sisters need to get to Springfield and find those relatives of yours as soon as you can. So we're going to get a wagon and some mules to pull it, and maybe some horses for you and Calvin and Luke, and I'm going to go with you and see that you get there safely."

Junie shook her head. "But, Skye, we don't have any money for a wagon—"

"Don't worry about that," Fargo said. "I've got enough for whatever you need."

"It was hard enough to get Calvin to agree to let you help us tonight. He's so proud . . . and he feels so guilty because he thinks he let Pa down. . . ."

"If he'd gotten in the middle of that, all he would have accomplished would have been to get himself killed, too," Fargo said bluntly.

"I know. But he doesn't see it that way, and he won't listen to reason."

"He'll have to. His responsibility now is to see to it that you and the others are safe."

"Well . . . maybe you can get him to go along with what you say."

Fargo hated to make her relive that horrible time any more than she already had, but there were still a few things he wanted to know.

"What happened the next morning?" he asked.

Junie swallowed hard. "We—we cut the bodies down. We couldn't get to them before that because it was still too hot out by the barn. The deputies helped us get them down and . . . and bury them. Pa was laid to rest beside my mother, and we put Mr. Tompkins and Mr. Curry and Bill Donner out there, too, since their families weren't anywhere around. The deputies promised that they'd get word to the families." Junie shook her head. "They said they were sure sorry about everything that had happened, but there wasn't anything anybody could do about it. We gathered up some food, and the deputies let us take blankets and quilts with us, too, even though they said they didn't have to." She shrugged. "Then we started walking."

"You're sure those relatives of yours in Springfield will take you in?"

"Pretty sure. Aunt Eula—she's my father's sister—lives there, and so does Aunt Geraldine. She was married to my uncle Fresnall, who was Pa's brother. Some of our cousins live down there, too." Junie's mouth quirked. "We're going to try to keep the family together, but it may not be possible. Some of us may have to split up and go live with different relatives. That'll take some arguing with Calvin, too. But we'll do what has to be done."

Fargo thought that was a good attitude for Junie to have, even though it was sad that things had come to that. He said, "I know some folks in Springfield, too, and they might be able to help out some if they need

59

to. We'll get you all settled and keep you together if we can."

"Thank you, Skye." Junie managed to smile. "I don't know where we'd be now if it wasn't for you. Freezing to death out in the woods, I imagine."

"At least you don't have to worry about that anymore." He put his arm around her again and snuggled her against him. "It's going to be all right."

They sat there together for a few minutes in an easy, companionable silence. But then Junie said tentatively, "Skye . . . when I finished telling you what—what happened, for a minute there you looked like you wanted . . . I don't know . . . you looked like you wanted to kill somebody."

"I was just sorry to hear what happened to you kids," Fargo said. That wasn't exactly a lie.

"Good. Because I was afraid . . . well, I was afraid from the way you looked, you wanted to ride up to Braxton's Lick and go after Black Hugo and Garrett and Joel. I wouldn't want you to do that. I wouldn't want you to get hurt."

"You don't reckon I can take care of myself?" Fargo asked dryly.

"Nobody can beat the Braxtons," Junie said in a hollow voice. "They're too evil."

Once he got the Haddon youngsters safely to Springfield, he would have to see about that, Fargo thought.

He sent Junie back to bed a short time later and stretched out on the bench to get some sleep himself. It was hard to doze off, though, because he kept seeing that horrible, bloody scene at the Haddon farm. And when he did finally fall asleep, his dreams were haunted by it. . . .

Fargo's iron constitution kept him from being too tired the next morning. He had just come in from checking on the Ovaro when Grundy stumbled out from the back to build up the fire and get some coffee on to boil.

"Mornin'," the roadhouse's proprietor mumbled as he saw Fargo come in the door, slapping his hands together to warm them. "What's the weather like out there?"

"Cold as a gravedigger's shovel," Fargo replied. "And there's some ice on the ground, but not too much."

Grundy shivered. He poked the fire up, put some wood on it, and stood there rubbing his hands together, trying to warm them.

"No more trouble last night?"

"Not a bit," Fargo said.

"I didn't think those boys would come back after the way you peppered them with lead."

While he was outside, Fargo had walked out into the woods where the bushwhackers had lurked, and he had found a good-sized bloodstain on the ground. From the looks of it, whoever he'd wounded had been hit pretty bad. That might have been enough to make the others think twice about coming after him again.

As Grundy turned away from the fireplace, he gave Fargo a leer and asked, "Lizbeth pay you a visit last night?"

"What makes you ask that?" Fargo replied coolly.

"I seen the way she was lookin' at you, like a pup that wants to lick its master's . . . hand. Don't you believe all the things she says, mister. That time in the barn . . . hell, it was more her idea than mine, and it wasn't like I was the first fella she'd lured in there, either, not by a long shot."

"Grundy?"

"Yeah?"

"Why don't you shut up and see about rustling some breakfast?"

Grundy didn't get mad. He just nodded and said, "Yeah, I can do that." He started toward the bar, but before going behind it he paused and looked at Fargo again, who was now standing in front of the fireplace. "You said your name is Skye Fargo?"

"That's right."

"I been thinkin' about that name. It sounded familiar. Finally came to me that you're the fella they call the Trailsman. Ain't that right?"

"It is," Fargo said.

"I thought as much. Copeland's lucky all you did was break his wrist. You could've killed all four of them."

Fargo didn't say anything, and after a few seconds Grundy just grunted and went on about his work.

When the coffee was ready, Fargo grasped the pot's handle with a thick piece of leather that sat near the hearth for that purpose, lifted it, and poured a cup for himself. He carried the steaming black brew over to the bar and said to Grundy, "Do you know of anybody around here who'd sell me a wagon and a team, and maybe a couple of saddle horses?"

"Maybe. How come you need a wagon?"

Fargo indulged the man's curiosity. "I'm going to take those youngsters down to Springfield and see that they get there safely."

Grundy let out a whistle. "Sounds like you *have* adopted them."

"They need somebody's help. I'm here, so I reckon I'm elected." Fargo didn't say anything about the story Junie had told him the night before—or what he planned to do once he had escorted them to Springfield.

"You're in luck. An old man who lives a couple o' miles north of here builds wagons and sells 'em, when he's not farming. Not much farm work goin' on this time of year, so he ought to have a wagon or two for sale."

"What's his name, and how do I find him?"

"Name of Wilkerson." Grundy gave Fargo directions for finding the farm. "He'll have mules, too, but they'll cost you a pretty penny. Wilkerson don't sell anything cheap."

"What about saddle horses?"

"Go over to the store and talk to Hank Merriman, who owns the place. He's got a little livery stable out back. You probably didn't see it when you came in last night, it bein' so dark and all."

Fargo hadn't seen the stable, but he was glad to hear that there was one in Bear Creek. He nodded and said, "I'm much obliged."

"Hell, it's the least I can do," Grundy said with a shrug. "Now that I know you're the Trailsman, I'm glad you didn't shoot me, too, on general principles."

"I thought about it," Fargo said.

He didn't know if Grundy believed him or not, but the man gave him a nervous look and moved off down the bar.

Grundy got out a frying pan and some bacon, and a big flat shovel for cooking johnnycake. A short time later the smell of the food cooking filled the roadhouse. Fargo wasn't surprised when the Haddon youngsters began stumbling out from the back. The aromas had drifted into their rooms and woken them. They hadn't had much to eat in the past week or so, and their bellies were insistent that they get up.

When Junie came into the main room, she looked at Fargo and smiled, then looked away suddenly. As her face reddened, Fargo knew she was remembering how she had stood naked in front of him and offered herself to him.

He kept his own expression neutral and hoped she

would get over her embarrassment. The way he saw it, she didn't have anything to be ashamed of.

Lizbeth didn't come out for breakfast, but Grundy wasn't worried about that. "She hardly ever stirs outta bed before noon," he explained.

He brought platters of johnnycake and bacon and cups of coffee over to the long table where everyone was seated. The children dug in eagerly. Junie tried to stop them, saying, "We haven't said grace yet." But when she saw the stricken looks they gave her, she relented and said, "Well, maybe the good Lord won't mind, this once."

There was a good deal of talk and laughter around the table as they ate. Even though the family had suffered a tragedy only a short time earlier, these children had the resilience of youth. Fargo was sure they still grieved for their father, but in their innocence they recognized the basic truth that life had to go on, despite their mourning.

As they were finishing up breakfast, Fargo sipped from his third cup of coffee and then announced, "I'm going to be traveling with you to Springfield."

Most of the youngsters looked happy about that, but Calvin's head came up and a frown appeared on his face.

"You reckon we can't take care of ourselves?" he asked sharply.

"I expect you can, but I'm going along anyway."

"We don't need anybody's help!"

Junie said, "Calvin, take it easy. We *do* need help, and you know it. And Mr. Fargo's being mighty generous to offer to give us a hand."

"You're just sweet on him!" Calvin accused angrily.

Hannah said, "Junie's got a beau! Junie's got a beau!" Sally and Arlo took up the chant until Junie silenced all three of them with a stern look.

"Calvin, there's no harm and no shame in letting somebody help you," Fargo said. "Like I told you last night, there'll come a time when you'll be able to pass along the favor to somebody else. That's the way life works . . . the way it ought to, anyway."

He outlined his plan to buy a wagon and team, along with some saddle horses. Calvin listened, but he had a dubious look on his face.

"We won't never be able to pay back all that money," he muttered when Fargo was finished.

"Nobody asked you to."

Calvin surprised Fargo a little then by nodding and saying, "All right. I'm not a damned fool—"

"Calvin," Junie said warningly.

"Yeah, I know, I know. I'm not supposed to cuss. But I know it's too far to walk. Likely we'd freeze or starve to death along the way. I sure don't like takin' charity . . . but I reckon we don't have a choice."

Fargo got to his feet. "I'm glad you see it that way. How about coming along with me to get the wagon and the team and the horses?"

Calvin looked surprised. "You want me to come with you?"

"I think it'd be a good idea. You're the head of this family now, aren't you?"

"Yeah, I guess so." Calvin stood up and squared his shoulders. "Yeah, I reckon I am."

"Come on, then," Fargo told him. "We're burning daylight."

They walked across the road to Merriman's Store, stepping around the patches of ice on the ground. The overcast of the day before was gone, but the winter sunlight was weak and watery. It was enough to show Fargo the barn and corrals behind the store. He and Calvin went inside.

Hank Merriman was a bald man with a prominent

Adam's apple. He reminded Fargo a little of a buzzard, but he was friendly and more than willing to sell the two saddle horses he had on hand in the stable.

Fargo would have liked to get a mount for Junie, too, but he figured she wouldn't mind riding on the wagon. Or that might be a better job for Luke, he reflected, depending on which one of them handled the mule team better. That could be decided later, once they were actually on their way.

The saddles Merriman had weren't very good, but they would do. Fargo bought them, too, and he and Calvin saddled up the horses. One was a brown gelding with white stockings, the other a rangy bay. Calvin seemed particularly taken with the bay, so Fargo said, "I reckon that one's yours."

"Really? I never had a horse of my own before."

"Life's going to be a lot different for you from here on out, Calvin. Harder in most ways, more than likely. But there's something to be said for growing up and taking on some responsibility. It comes to every man sooner or later."

"So does death," Calvin said, his expression growing bleak again, no doubt because of the memories that came flooding back.

"I can't argue with that," Fargo said. "Wouldn't do a damn bit of good if I did."

That brought a chuckle from Calvin. "Better not talk like that around Junie," he warned.

"I'll try not to," Fargo said solemnly.

They led the horses over to the roadhouse and tied the reins to the hitch rail out front. Fargo was ready to head up to the Wilkerson farm to see about buying that wagon, but he wanted to let Junie know where he and Calvin were going. They went inside.

Junie and the children sat near the fireplace, enjoying the warmth. Fargo knew that once a person got chilled to bone, it seemed to take a long time to really warm up again.

Fargo was about to explain what the plan was, when suddenly a shout came from outside. "Fargo!" a man bellowed angrily. "Fargo, get out here, damn you, and keep your hands where we can see 'em!"

As if to punctuate the command, a woman's scream rang out, cutting shrilly through the cold morning air.

Behind the bar, Grundy stiffened in alarm. "That sounded like Lizbeth!" he said as he reached under the bar for his shotgun.

"Stay here," Fargo snapped at Calvin, Junie, and the other youngsters. He swung toward the door and moved quickly through it onto the porch.

Two of the men he had clashed with the night before stood there in the trail in front of the roadhouse. One of them had his arm looped around Lizbeth's neck, holding her tightly against him. The other man stood to one side, a rifle in his hands.

Lizbeth's light brown hair was tousled and the thin sleeping gown she wore was disheveled. From the looks of things, the men had gotten into her room somehow and dragged her out without making any noise about it. Lizbeth was probably cold in the flimsy garment, but that was the least of her worries right now.

The man who held her had the barrel of a gun pressed cruelly against the side of her head.

"Don't you make a move for your gun, Fargo," the man warned. "I'll splatter this slut's brains all over the road if you do."

"Take it easy," Fargo said. Even though his heart slugged heavily in his chest, he kept his face and voice calm. He had to remain cool and steady if he was going to have any hope of getting Lizbeth out of this alive. He went on, "There's no need to hurt her. Let her go, and we'll settle this between us, the way it ought to be."

Lizbeth's captor snorted in contempt. "Like hell. We know who you are. You're the Trailsman. We ain't gonna gunfight with you. We're just gonna kill you."

"Like you killed Wilbur!" the second man put in. "You broke Luther's wrist, and then you shot Wilbur in the guts!"

"Only because he was trying to shoot me," Fargo pointed out. He didn't expect reasoning with these hombres to do any good, but at least they hadn't started shooting yet.

"You had it comin'," the first man snarled. Abruptly, he called, "Grundy! I see you back there, you fat little son of a bitch! Come out from behind Fargo."

Grundy stepped out onto the porch, moving to Fargo's left. "If you hurt Lizbeth, I'll kill you," he said. His face was pale over the dark beard, and he looked scared but determined. He had the shotgun in his hands.

Both of the men laughed. "You don't scare us, you little weasel," the second one said. "You ain't got the guts to do anything."

"Try me," Grundy warned.

"Nobody needs to try anything," Fargo said quickly, wanting to avoid a shoot-out if possible, especially while Lizbeth was in the line of fire. To Sandon and Lindsey—he didn't know which one was which—he went on. "You know you won't get away with it if you hurt that woman."

The man with the gun to her head laughed harshly. "Nobody's gonna care what happens to some whore."

"I care," Fargo corrected him. "I'll kill you. You

68

know I can do it. But if you let her go and walk away, that'll be the end of it. Nobody else has to die."

"Don't listen to him, Lindsey," the man with the rifle said. He started to lift the weapon. "I'm gonna shoot him now!"

"Wait!" Lindsey said urgently. He frowned, and Fargo could tell that he was starting to get worried. "Fargo's right. If we kill Lizbeth, then we got nothin' to bargain with."

"Well, it's her own fault!" Sandon said. "She started it by bein' snippy to Luther. If she'd gone with him when he said to, none o' this would've happened."

"Yeah, but Luther didn't have to hit her, no matter how she acted. That's what got Fargo mixed up in this."

Sandon was getting confused. "Now you're sayin' it's Luther's fault?" The barrel of the rifle dipped slightly toward the ground.

"All I'm sayin' is maybe we didn't think this through good enough."

Neither of them was very smart, Fargo realized. They operated more on instinct than brains, and instinct told them they had to settle the score for the injured Copeland and the dead Wilbur. Lindsey was just smart enough to start thinking that it might not be worth it.

"Hell with this," Sandon muttered. "Thinkin' too much makes my head hurt."

He jerked the rifle up and fired.

Fargo had seen the telltale tensing of Sandon's muscles and the flare of murderous fury in the man's eyes. He was already throwing himself to the side as smoke and flame geysered from the barrel of the weapon. His Colt was in his hand as he landed on his right side and triggered off two fast shots.

The slugs smacked into Sandon's chest and lifted him up and back, completely off his feet. The rifle flew out of his hands as he crashed to the ground.

With a shouted curse, Lindsey pulled his gun away from Lizbeth's head and fired at Fargo instead. The bullet hit the porch and kicked up splinters that stung Fargo's cheek. He couldn't return the fire because Lindsey still held Lizbeth in front of him as a human shield.

At that moment, however, she was able to lower her head and sink her teeth into his arm. He let out a howl of pain and loosened his grip. She twisted free and ran to the side.

Lindsey tried to bring his pistol around toward Grundy, but he was too late. The shotgun in Grundy's hands roared. The range was close enough so that the double charge of buckshot didn't have much time to spread before it tore into Lindsey's chest and turned it into a bloody ruin. Lindsey was driven backward by the fatal impact.

But he still had his gun in his hand, and it blasted out a shot as Lindsey's death throes made his trigger finger contract. Grundy grunted and took an involuntary step backward. His back hit the wall of the road-house, and he slowly slid down it into a sitting position. The empty greener slipped out of his fingers.

"Grundy!" Lizbeth screamed. She threw herself onto the porch and dropped to her knees beside him.

Fargo surged to his feet and stepped down into the road. He kept his Colt trained on Sandon as he approached the man. He was pretty sure Sandon was dead, but taking unnecessary chances was a good way to get killed on the frontier.

Sandon was dead, all right, his eyes staring sightlessly at the pale blue winter sky. Fargo went over to

Lindsey. There was no real reason to check on him other than habitual caution. That double charge of buckshot had blown a huge hole through his chest. His heart and most of his lungs were splattered over the street behind him.

Fargo holstered the revolver as he turned toward the roadhouse. People were emerging from Merriman's Store, drawn by the shots, but Fargo ignored them. He stepped up onto the porch and asked, "How're you doing, Grundy?"

The proprietor looked up at him, eyes wide with pain and amazement. "I'm shot," he said simply. He had his hand pressed to his right side. When he took it away and looked at it, the palm was covered with blood. He said again, "I'm shot."

"Oh, my God, do something!" Lizbeth wailed. "Can't you help him?"

Fargo knelt beside Grundy and pulled the man's shirt up, out of his trousers. As Fargo lifted the blood-stained garment, he saw that the bullet Lindsey had fired as his last act on earth had plowed a shallow furrow in Grundy's right side, about four inches above his waist.

The wound was messy but probably not serious. If it was cleaned up and Grundy took it easy for a while, the injury ought to heal.

"You'll live," Fargo said with a smile. "At least, that scratch isn't going to kill you."

"Scratch!" Lizbeth repeated indignantly. "He's wounded!"

"That's right, and we need to get him inside and pour whiskey over the wound. Then you can wrap some bandages around him."

"I can do that," Lizbeth said with an eager nod. "I'll help any way I can."

Fargo looked at the doorway. Calvin and Luke stood there, looking out at the scene of the gunfight with wide eyes. Junie was right behind them.

"You two boys give me a hand," Fargo told Calvin and Luke. "I'll get his shoulders, and you get his feet."

Working together, Fargo and the two youngsters lifted Grundy and carried him into the roadhouse. They laid him on one of the tables.

"Careful," Grundy warned between gritted teeth. "Don't get too much blood on the table. It's hell to get out."

"You let me worry about that," Lizbeth told him. "I reckon I'll be running this place while you're laid up, so it's my concern, not yours, and I don't care about a little blood."

Grundy looked up at her. "You're gonna . . . keep the place goin' for me?"

"Of course. What did you expect?"

Grundy shook his head. "I dunno. Maybe that you hoped I'd bleed to death."

"Oh, hush," she said. "Don't be a damned fool."

While they were looking at each other, Fargo turned to the Haddon youngsters and asked, "Is everybody all right?"

Junie nodded. "We're fine."

"Good. I was afraid a stray slug might've come in here and hit one of you. That's why I didn't want any shooting. Those two didn't give me much choice in the matter, though."

"I never saw shootin' like that, Mr. Fargo," Luke said in an awed voice.

Calvin said, "Aw, I could do that, if I had a good gun and a chance to practice with it."

"You could not!" Luke objected.

"You don't know that!"

Fargo left them squabbling, trusting to Junie not to

let things get too out of hand. He turned his attention back to the wounded Grundy. Getting a bottle of whiskey from behind the bar, he said, "This is going to hurt, but it'll keep that graze from festering."

"Go ahead, Fargo," Grundy said through lips that were already clenched against the pain.

Fargo poured the fiery liquor over the bullet furrow. Grundy gritted his teeth and moaned between them. A moment later he relaxed as the pain began to subside.

"Maybe you've got a petticoat or something you can tear into strips for bandages," Fargo suggested to Lizbeth.

She reached down for the hem of her gown. "This'll do."

Fargo stopped her from pulling the garment up and over her head. "Maybe you can find something better in your room."

She shrugged and said, "I'll go look." She leaned over Grundy and asked in a tender voice, "You'll be all right until I get back?"

"Yeah. I'll . . . be fine. Thanks . . . Lizbeth."

She patted him on the shoulder. "You rest easy, honey. I'll take good care of you."

Grundy smiled.

So did Fargo as he turned away and slowly shook his head. You never knew what it might take to get folks' true feelings for each other to come out. But once they did, things were never the same.

He had a feeling that for Grundy and Lizbeth, what they had discovered on this violent morning might be worth a little blood and danger.

5

Once Grundy was patched up and put to bed and Lizbeth was dressed, Fargo talked to her long enough to discover that his guess had been correct: Lindsey and Sandon had climbed into her room through the window, grabbed her and clapped a hand over her mouth to keep her from calling for help, and taken her out and around the building to the front to serve as the bait in the trap for Fargo.

That trap had caught them instead, and now Hank Merriman, who also served as Bear Creek's undertaker as well as its storekeeper and liveryman, had loaded the bodies on a wagon and taken them around behind his place. They would be buried without much ceremony in the graveyard beside the church. Later, Merriman would drive out to the squalid cabin shared by the four men and see if Wilbur's body was there.

Fargo didn't much care one way or the other. He had other things to occupy his mind. He and Calvin mounted up and rode out of Bear Creek, heading north toward Wilkerson's farm.

The old man had been busy over the winter. He had four wagons parked in his big barn, all of them for sale. Only one already had a canvas cover stretched over its back, however, so after a little dickering, Fargo bought that one, along with a team of six mules to pull it.

The price was high and took a lot of the money in Fargo's poke, but he figured he could sell the wagon and mules in Springfield and get most, if not all, of his investment back. It would take only a week or so for him and the Haddon youngsters to get there. Those young'uns would be a lot better off traveling in the wagon than trying to walk.

Fargo and Calvin tied their horses to the back of the wagon and climbed onto the seat once the team was hitched up. Fargo handed the reins to Calvin.

"You want me to handle the team?" the youngster asked in surprise.

"I expect you've driven a wagon before, since you grew up on a farm."

"Well, yeah, plenty of times, but—"

Fargo waved a hand at the mules. "Get 'em moving, then."

Calvin grinned, slapped the leathers against the backs of the mules, and yelled lustily at the animals until they broke into a steady walk. The wagon was sturdily built, the wheels were well lubricated, and it rolled easily down the road.

"You and I will be riding ahead of the wagon once we get started to Springfield," Fargo explained. "Who do you reckon would do a better job of driving the wagon, Junie or Luke?"

"Junie," Calvin said without hesitation. He grinned. "She can yell at mules even louder than me. She won't cuss, though, like a regular mule skinner, so she makes up words to call 'em. You ought to hear some of the stuff she comes up with."

"I reckon I will," Fargo said.

"She's sweet on you, you know. I can tell."

"Well, you just keep that to yourself."

"You—you wouldn't do anything to make her sad, would you, Mr. Fargo?"

"I sure don't intend to," Fargo said truthfully. He knew, though, that good intentions were sometimes hard to live up to.

They got back to Bear Creek in short order, and the children were full of questions and shouted comments as they came tumbling out of the roadhouse to look at their new conveyance. Fargo told Luke to keep an eye on them and then motioned for Junie and Calvin to follow him as he walked over to Merriman's Store.

Hammering came from out back. Fargo figured Merriman was knocking together a couple of crude coffins for Lindsey and Sandon. Merriman's buxom wife was behind the counter, though, and she was more than happy to start putting together an order of supplies for the trip. Paying for them was going to just about clean Fargo out, but he didn't mention that to Calvin and Junie.

While the supplies were being gathered, Fargo walked over to a glass-topped case and looked into it. Several revolvers were displayed in the case. He looked speculatively at Calvin for a moment, then called Mrs. Merriman over.

"I'll take that Colt Navy revolver, if I like the balance of it," he told her.

"Of course." She took the gun from the case and handed it to him. Fargo hefted it, tested the balance, checked the action.

Nodding in satisfaction, he said, "I'll need a box of ammunition for it, too, and a holster, if you've got one." His Colt was a .44; the Navy model was a .36 caliber.

"We'll get you fixed right up," Mrs. Merriman said.

She glanced at Fargo's hip. "You've already got a gun, though."

"It's not for me," Fargo said.

Once the storekeeper's wife had given him the ammunition and holster, Fargo carried everything over to Calvin, whose eyes widened in surprise as Fargo handed him the holstered gun.

"I hope we don't run into any more trouble," Fargo said, "but in case we do, you need something better than that old flintlock pistol. This is a good dependable weapon. You know how to load it?"

"I—I think so," Calvin said, running his hand over the revolver's grip. "A fella up around home had one, and I saw him loadin' it sometimes."

"Show me."

Fumbling only slightly, Calvin loaded five of the chambers. Fargo stopped him when he started to load the sixth one.

"You want to leave that one empty and let the hammer rest on it while you're carrying the gun, so it doesn't go off by accident. The only time you load six is when you're already in a fight, or you know you're about to be in one."

Calvin nodded. "I'll remember."

"See how the belt fits."

Calvin strapped on the gun belt. The holster hung too low at first, so Fargo had him adjust it. "You're gonna have to show me how to draw as fast as you," the youngster said.

"You don't have to draw fast. You just want to be able to get the gun out fairly quickly without dropping it. Staying calm and being able to hit what you're shooting at is a lot more important than speed."

Calvin nodded, but he didn't look totally convinced. Like most young men who strapped on a six-shooter for the first time, he was probably thinking of the stories he had heard about gunfights—most of which weren't true.

Calvin walked out onto the store's front porch and started practicing drawing the gun. Junie watched him through the big window and frowned. She glanced over at Fargo. "Are you sure that was a good idea?"

"Giving him the gun, you mean? Better for him to have something like that, rather than the single-shot pistol he's been carrying around."

"Wouldn't it be better for us to have a rifle, so that we can use it to shoot game if we need to?"

She had a point there. Fargo dug in his pocket and came up with the last of his money. He used it for a single-shot carbine that was hanging on the wall of the store.

"You can keep it in the wagon," he told Junie. "Can you shoot?"

"Of course I can," she answered a little indignantly. "I could knock a squirrel out of a tree when I was ten years old!"

"Good to know," Fargo said with a grin.

When their order was ready, Fargo paid for it, then called Calvin inside. He, Calvin, and Junie carried the boxes of supplies to the wagon. They had enough provisions to get them to Springfield, although as Junie had mentioned, it would help if they could get some game along the way for fresh meat. At this time of year, that might not be possible.

"Everybody ready to go?" Fargo asked. He got a chorus of agreement from the youngsters.

He went back into the roadhouse to say good-bye to Lizbeth and Grundy. They were both in Grundy's room. Lizbeth was feeding him some soup.

"Take good care of him," Fargo told her with a smile.

"I intend to," she said.

"Thanks, Fargo," Grundy said.

"Thanks for what? I'm the one who sort of brought down this trouble on you, Grundy."

"I don't mind." Grundy looked at Lizbeth. "Don't mind at all."

Fargo ran a thumb along his bearded jawline. "Don't I recollect you saying something about the two of you being cousins?"

"Second cousins," Grundy said, "or is it third?"

"Third, I think," Lizbeth said. "Once or twice removed. I never could keep up with that."

"Anyway," Grundy said with a laugh, "most folks up here in the mountains are related one way or another, ain't they?"

Fargo just shook his head and left them with a wave and a grin.

A couple of minutes later, the wagon rolled south out of Bear Creek, with Junie at the reins and Fargo and Calvin riding ahead. Luke rode the other saddle horse and stayed beside the wagon. The rest of the children were packed into the back, crowded around behind Junie so they could see where they were going.

The temperature didn't warm much during the day, despite the sunshine. The cold didn't dampen the mood of the travelers, though. A lot of laughter came from the wagon, and Fargo figured that was a good thing for those youngsters to experience, after all the tragedy they had been through.

Every time they stopped to rest the mule team, Calvin wanted to practice with the revolver Fargo had bought for him. Finally, Fargo gave in to his pleas and walked with him about a hundred yards up a hill.

"This ought to be far enough away from the wagon," Fargo said as he came to a stop.

"What do you think I'm gonna do, accidentally

shoot one of my brothers or sisters?" Calvin demanded.

"Not up here you won't." Fargo pointed. "See that dead tree over yonder? Try to hit it."

Calvin faced the tree, which was only about thirty feet away. He took a deep breath and then snatched at the butt of the gun, trying to pull it fast from the holster.

"Damn it!" he exclaimed as the Colt Navy almost slipped out of his fingers. He had to grab it with his other hand to keep it from falling to the ground.

"See why I told you not to worry about a fast draw? If that tree was fixing to shoot at you, you'd be dead now."

"All right, all right," Calvin grumbled. "I understand. Let me try again."

Fargo waved a hand. "Have at it."

Calvin pouched the iron and took his stance again. This time he drew much more slowly, but the gun was under control as he raised it and thumbed back the hammer. He paused only a split second to draw a bead, then pulled the trigger. The Colt boomed and bucked in his hand.

"Did I hit it?" he asked eagerly as he fanned his free hand at the cloud of smoke that had come from the barrel.

"Does it look like it?"

Calvin's eyes searched the gray trunk of the dead tree. He didn't see any fresh marks on it.

"Damn!"

"Try again," Fargo said.

Shots rang out, slowly and somewhat irregularly, as Calvin continued his target practice. Finally, when splinters had flown from the tree three shots in a row, Fargo called a halt.

"You're doing a lot better, but you don't want to

waste ammunition. You can practice some more later."

"All right," Calvin said. "Thanks, Mr. Fargo—"

The youngster started to turn away, but he froze suddenly as a rustling sounded in the brush nearby. Fargo heard it, too, and thought the noise was probably made by some small animal.

A second later that guess was proven wrong, as a man stood up from the bushes, pointed an ancient muzzle-loading rifle at them, and said, "Don't move or I'll let daylight through you!"

The man was sort of ancient himself, Fargo saw. A white beard jutted out from his jaw, and white hair hung from beneath the shapeless old hat crammed on his head. He wore overalls and a coat that looked like it had been made from the skin of a bear.

"Take it easy, old-timer," Fargo said as he held his hands well away from his gun. He didn't want to spook the old man into firing.

Calvin still held his new Colt Navy, and what Fargo saw in the youngster's eyes was troubling. He could tell that Calvin was thinking about jerking the gun up and threatening the old-timer.

"Don't do it, Calvin," Fargo ordered in a low, hard voice. "You'll just get yourself killed."

Fargo had seen how steady the barrel of the rifle was. The man holding it might be old, but he still had plenty of bark on him. He wasn't one to take chances with.

"Best listen to your friend and put that shootin' iron back in your holster, younker," the old man said. "Do it slow and careful-like, though. I'm a crazy old galoot, and it wouldn't take much to make me shoot you."

"All right, all right," Calvin muttered. Slowly, he slid the Colt back in the holster on his hip.

Fargo glanced down the hill at the wagon and the

rest of the Haddon youngsters. None of them seemed to have noticed this confrontation on the hill. Fargo hoped that remained the case. He didn't want any of them interfering and getting hurt.

"Now," the old man said, "tell me how come you folks are followin' me."

"Followin' you?" Calvin burst out. "We never even seen you before, mister! Why in blazes would we be followin' you?"

" 'Cause you're after my gold, that's why!" The old man came closer. Fargo could tell now that he was short, only a little over five feet tall. "Folks been tryin' to kill me and take my gold for years. Why should you be any different? I want you to admit it 'fore I ventilate you, though."

"There's not any gold mines in Missouri," Fargo pointed out.

"Didn't say I got it in Missouri, now did I?" The old-timer laughed. "Brung it back from Californy, I did. Went out there in forty-nine with all the other argonauts, and I done struck it rich. Folks been tryin' to steal my fortune from me ever since I come back home."

The old-timer's wild-eyed expression made Fargo wonder if he was completely right in the head. It was entirely possible that he didn't have any gold, from California or otherwise.

But if he believed that he did, and if he was equally convinced that somebody was after it, he could still be quite dangerous. Fargo needed to persuade the old man that he and the Haddons weren't any threat to him.

"We don't know anything about any gold, mister," Fargo told him. "This boy and his brothers and sisters are on their way to Springfield, and I'm riding along with them to make sure they get there safely."

"You ain't thieves?" the old man asked with a suspicious glare.

Fargo shook his head. "Not at all."

The old man jabbed the rifle barrel at them. "What's your names?"

"I'm Skye Fargo, and this is Calvin Haddon."

"Fargo, Fargo," the old man mused. "The feller they call the Trailsman?"

Maybe having a sometimes unwanted reputation was going to come in handy this time. "That's right," Fargo said.

"I never heard nothin' about the Trailsman bein' a crook." The rifle barrel lowered slightly. "You gimme your word you ain't after my gold?"

"You have my word on it," Fargo assured him.

"Well, in that case . . ." The old man pointed the rifle at the ground. The crazed gleam had gone out of his eyes. "Sorry for bein' so jumpy. A man gets that way when he has to worry about thieves all the time."

"I expect so," Fargo agreed.

The old-timer stepped forward and held out a gnarled hand. "Name's Strickland, front handle of Bowdoin, like that there college back east. Most folks just call me Bodie, though."

Fargo shook hands with the man. "Pleased to meet you, Bodie."

"Sorry about pointin' my rifle at you, younker," Bodie said as he shook with Calvin.

Calvin still looked leery of the old man, but he muttered, "That's all right."

Bodie looked at Fargo again. "Headin' for Springfield, you say?"

"That's right. They have relatives down there they're going to stay with."

"What happened to their folks?"

"We're orphans," Calvin answered. "Our ma got

sick and died a few years ago, and our pa—" He had to stop for a moment and drag a deep breath into his body before he could finish. "Our pa was lynched."

Bodie's rheumy eyes widened. "Lynched, you say! Was he an owlhooter?"

"He was an honest man!" Calvin said hotly. "They said he stole some cows, but he never did. The only reason it happened was so Black Hugo Braxton could get his hands on our land!"

"Braxton," Bodie said with a frown. "I've heard tell of him, and ain't none o' what I've heard been good, neither. You want to watch out for that ol' he-coon, boy." Tugging at his beard, Bodie added, "I reckon I ain't tellin' you nothin' you don't already know, though."

Fargo said, "That's why we're going to Springfield."

"On my way there myself. Got a daughter down there I ain't seen for a heap o' years, and since I'm gettin' old, I thought I might better pay her a visit whilst I still can." Bodie got a thoughtful look on his weathered old face. "Wouldn't be wantin' some company on the trip, now would you?"

Fargo wasn't sure how good an idea it would be to let the old man travel with them. From what he had seen of Bodie so far, the old-timer was prone to fits of suspicious anger. He might pose a danger to the children.

On the other hand, if they ran into any trouble, Bodie would be one more person who could help them. It might be worth a try, Fargo decided.

He was going to keep a pretty close eye on the old man, though.

"I reckon it would be all right," he said. "What do you think, Calvin?"

The youngster shrugged. "I don't really care, as long

as he doesn't go out of his head and try to shoot some of us."

"That ain't gonna happen," Bodie promised. "I know I'm amongst friends now."

"See that you remember," Fargo warned him.

"Don't you worry." Bodie tilted his rifle over his shoulder. "Lemme go get my mule."

He turned and vanished into the brush again, only to emerge a few moments later leading a big, raw-boned mule wearing an old saddle. A couple leather saddlebags, cracked and stained with age, were slung over the mule's back.

Bodie had a sort of gaunt, wolfish look about him, and Fargo wondered if the old-timer was running low on supplies. That might be one reason why he wanted to travel to Springfield with them.

They could afford to share their food with the old man, Fargo supposed. Maybe he wouldn't eat much.

They started down the hill toward the wagon. Jonas noticed that Fargo and Calvin had somebody else with them, and he shouted the news. Everyone gathered around Junie, who came out to meet Fargo, Calvin, and Bodie.

"Who's this?" she asked bluntly.

Fargo performed the introductions. Bodie yanked his hat off and made a rough little bow to Junie. "It's an honor to meet you, missy," he said. "I swear, the sight o' such a pretty gal is enough to warm up this cold winter day for an old pelican like me!"

Junie didn't look particularly flattered, but she said, "Thank you, Mr. Strickland."

"Land's sake, call me Bodie! All you young'uns can call me that."

"We were raised to be respectful of our elders," Junie insisted. "We'll call you Mr. Strickland."

"Well, I'm elder than just about anybody in these parts, so you do whatever you want, missy." Bodie got a sly look on his face. "You, uh, wouldn't happen to have an ol' stale biscuit or somethin' like that in that wagon, would you?" The question seemed to confirm Fargo's earlier guess about the old man's lack of supplies. "It's been a while since I et."

"As a matter of fact, we do still have a few biscuits left," Junie said. "Hannah, fetch Mr. Strickland a biscuit."

The younger girl hurried to carry out the order.

"What was all the shooting about, up there on the hill?" Junie asked Fargo.

"Just letting Calvin get a little practice with his new gun," he replied.

With a smile on his face, Calvin said, "I got pretty good, too."

"Is that true, Skye?"

"Well," Fargo said with a smile on his face, "if he keeps it up, he'll be less likely to shoot himself, rather than what he's aiming at." At Calvin's crestfallen look, he added, "You did just fine for the first time."

A short time later they got started again, with Fargo and Calvin riding out front along with Bodie now, who gnawed happily on the biscuit with his few remaining teeth.

Quietly, so that Junie and the others wouldn't hear, Fargo asked the old-timer, "What have you heard about Hugo Braxton?"

"Just that he's the big skookum he-wolf up there around Braxton's Lick. Folks say that when he was younger, he killed a bunch o' fellas from a family him and the other Braxtons was feudin' with . . ." Bodie looked over at Calvin. "Say, I recollect the other family was named Haddon, just like you."

"We're the last of the Haddons," Calvin said. "The last ones who lived around Braxton's Lick, anyway. Black Hugo decided he wanted my father's land, so he made it look like Pa stole those cows, and then his sons Garrett and Joel and their friends strung him up."

"Lord, have mercy! That's a terrible thing. When'd it happen?"

"A little over a week ago," Calvin replied solemnly.

"That recent? I'm plumb sorry, boy. I didn't have no idea you was still grievin'."

"I'm gonna do more than grieve," Calvin said. "One of these days, I'm gonna settle the score with Black Hugo and those bastard sons of his."

Fargo had been expecting to hear Calvin say something like that, but he was disappointed anyway. "That's not a good idea, Calvin," he said. "You'll get hurt or killed, and it won't change a thing."

"Yeah," Bodie said, "much as it hurts, sometimes there ain't nothin' you can do."

"Is that right? Well, what would you do?" Calvin challenged. "If your family was murdered, would you just sit back and do nothin'?"

Fargo's jaw tightened. He had endured tragedy in his own life, and he *hadn't* sat back and done nothing, as Calvin put it. He knew what it was like to ride for revenge. But he hadn't had a bunch of siblings depending on him, either.

"Once we get to Springfield, we'll talk about what to do next," he promised. "I know you don't want to just let it go, Calvin. I can't say as I blame you."

That mollified Calvin a little. They rode on in silence for a while.

Even though the sunlight wasn't very warm, it was strong enough to melt most of the sleet that had fallen the night before. Only a few icy patches were left, and they were in the shade of the pine trees that lined the road. The trail itself was clear.

Junie didn't push the mules too hard. As nightfall approached, Fargo figured they had come between eight and ten miles from Bear Creek. Not bad for the first day, he decided. They might do a little better in the days to come, as Junie got more used to handling the team.

When he spotted a likely-looking clearing not far from the road, he turned the Ovaro, pointed to the spot, and told Junie, "Drive up in there. We'll make camp for the night."

She nodded and hauled on the reins. "Gee!" she called out, using the term mule skinners employed to tell their teams to turn right. "Gee, you jug-headed frammiswallopers! Over there, you good-for-nothing doodlewhackers!"

Fargo smiled. He had been listening to Junie all day, and he didn't think she'd appreciate it if he told her that her made-up words often sounded more obscene than the usual cussing that mule skinners did.

Bodie didn't know the story behind Junie's yelling. With a puzzled frown on his face, he asked, "What language is that the gal's hollerin' in? Is it Comanche? Or Rooshian?"

Calvin chuckled. "It's pure Junie."

Fargo reined in and turned the Ovaro to look back along the road. The pine-covered hills through which they had been winding all day rose darkly behind them.

And in the fading daylight, Fargo saw a column of smoke rising, too. The wind had died down to almost nothing, so the black smoke climbed toward the sky in a pillar.

Fargo couldn't be sure, but he thought that the

place where the smoke originated was pretty close to the location of Bear Creek. That was troublesome. Somebody might be burning some brush or something like that, he told himself.

Usually, though, black smoke meant a building on fire. Fargo turned to look at the wagon, which Junie had pulled to a stop in the clearing. The younger children jumped down from it, glad to be stopped so that they could run around and play for a while.

Fargo thought about riding back up to Bear Creek to see what, if anything, was going on, but he had promised to help these youngsters and he couldn't abandon them. Such a trip would take most of the night.

Besides, if anything had happened at Bear Creek, it was too late for him to do anything about it. The trouble was already over. The smoke climbing into the sky was proof of that.

He hitched the Ovaro into a walk and rode into the clearing. As he swung down from the saddle, he pulled the Henry rifle from its sheath. He was going to keep the Henry with him tonight, and it might be a good idea to post a guard, too.

While Calvin and Luke were unhitching the mules and Junie and Hannah started gathering wood for a fire, Fargo drew Bodie Strickland aside and said to the old-timer, "There may be some trouble following these youngsters."

Bodie looked at him shrewdly. "Braxton trouble, you mean?"

"Hugo Braxton set it up so that everything looked legal about him taking over the Haddon land. But maybe after a while he decided he didn't want those children going off somewhere else and talking about what happened."

"You think he'd harm the young'uns?" Bodie

sounded like he found it hard to believe that anybody could be that low.

"I don't know," Fargo said honestly. "I don't know anything about Braxton except what Junie and Calvin have told me. But if he's hated the Haddon family for so long and killed some of them in the past, who's to say he might not decide to make a clean slate of it?"

Bodie ran his fingers over the smooth stock of his old rifle. "I know I'm a cantankerous sort, and some even say I'm a mite touched in the head sometimes . . . but I don't hold with hurtin' young'uns. If it comes to a fight, Fargo, count me in."

Fargo nodded. "That's what I hoped you'd say. Think you might be up to standing a turn on guard duty tonight?"

"Damn right."

"I saw some smoke, back toward the place we came from," Fargo added, inclining his head toward the north. "I don't know if it means a thing, but I reckon we ought to be careful until we find out."

"Yeah, I reckon so." Bodie nodded toward Calvin. "You gonna tell the boy?"

"Not yet."

"I seen him shootin' earlier. That's what drew me to you folks. He ain't ready for a real fight, not hardly."

"No, he's not," Fargo agreed, "but sometimes a fight comes to a fella, whether he's ready for it or not."

6

A fire, decent food, and a wagon to ride in so that they didn't have to trudge wearily along all day made a huge difference in the Haddon youngsters. When Fargo had first encountered them the day before, all seven of them had been pale, drawn, and haunted. Now color had returned to their faces and life to their eyes. They felt sorrow for what had happened in the past, but they felt hope for the future, too.

Arlo and Sally began to get tired as soon as they had eaten supper. Junie took them into the wagon and bedded them down in the back. Then Jonas and Hannah began nodding and having trouble keeping their eyes open. They climbed into the back of the wagon, too, to roll up in their blankets.

That left Junie, Calvin, and Luke sitting beside the fire, along with Fargo and Bodie.

"Where are you going to sleep, Skye?" Junie asked.

"Figured Bodie and I would spread our bedrolls under the wagon," Fargo said. He didn't mention that only one of them would be sleeping at a time. The other one would be on guard.

"There's room for everybody inside," Junie said. "It might be a little crowded, but we can all squeeze in."

Bodie chuckled. "Missy, that's a mite too civilized

for me. I been sleepin' outdoors for so long that even in a wagon I'd be likely to start feelin' cooped up."

"And I'll be fine, too," Fargo added. "With the sky cleared off and the winds dying down, it'll be mighty cold by morning, but Bodie and I will keep the fire fed overnight. We should all be pretty snug."

"Well, if you're sure . . ."

"Go ahead and turn in whenever you're ready," Fargo told her. "Don't worry about us."

Calvin commented, "I didn't get to practice my shootin' anymore."

"Time for that in the morning, maybe," Fargo said.

"I ought to have a gun, too," Luke said. "I'm fourteen. That's old enough to carry a shootin' iron."

"You don't need a gun," Calvin scoffed. "You're just a kid."

"Yeah, well, so are you."

"Am not! I'm a man full growed."

Fargo and Bodie exchanged an amused glance. Squabbling like that tended to disprove the very point that Calvin was making—but the youngster wouldn't see it that way, of course.

"Come on, you two," Junie said with a smile. "Let's get some sleep. We'll make an early start in the morning and get even farther toward Springfield tomorrow."

"That sounds like a good idea to me," Fargo said.

Still grumbling and muttering at each other, Calvin and Luke climbed into the wagon. Junie hesitated, looking back at Fargo and saying, "Skye . . . ?"

"What is it?"

She turned and came over to him as he stood up from the log where he had been sitting. "I just . . . After the past week or so, it's hard for me to believe that we've got this wagon, and plenty of supplies, and it's all thanks to you. So I just wanted to tell you how much I appreciate it."

"You're mighty welcome," he told her.

Junie licked her lips. Fargo had a feeling that if Bodie hadn't been sitting right there, she might have kissed him.

At this moment, he wasn't sure if he was glad they had run into the old-timer or not . . .

"Well," Junie said after a few seconds, "good night, Skye."

"Night, Junie."

Without looking back this time, she climbed into the wagon. Fargo could hear some moving around inside the vehicle as all of the Haddon youngsters got settled for the night. Then the clearing was silent except for the crackling of the fire.

Quietly, Bodie commented, "For a gal who was raised to respect her elders, that one's mighty quick to call you by your Christian name, Fargo."

Fargo didn't respond to that. He just said, "You want to stand guard first or second, old man?"

"Second's fine by me. I tend to wake up along after midnight, anyway. One o' the hazards o' gettin' old, I reckon."

Bodie had a buffalo robe instead of blankets. He unrolled it under the wagon, crawled onto it, and wrapped it snugly around him. Within a few minutes, soft snores came from the old man.

Fargo sat close to the fire for a while, feeding broken branches into the flames until the blaze was burning well. He was careful not to look directly into the fire. That ruined a man's night vision, and if there was trouble lurking out there in the shadows, Fargo wanted to be able to see it.

He stood up and faded into the woods, taking the

Henry rifle with him. The fire could be seen easily from the road. He felt a little twinge of guilt at what he was doing. It felt like he was using those children as bait in a trap—and when you got right down to it, that was right.

But he didn't want trouble dogging their trail all the way to Springfield. If someone was following them, Fargo wanted to draw whoever it was out into the open now.

He found a large rock in a particularly deep shadow and sat down on it to wait. This far away from the fire, the woods were very cold, and the chill seeped into Fargo's bones. He ignored the discomfort. His senses were all on edge, alert for any sign of trouble.

An hour passed slowly, then two. Fargo stood up and stretched from time to time to keep his muscles from getting too stiff. It was during one of those stretches that he heard a faint clink and recognized it as the sound of a horseshoe hitting a rock.

Instantly, Fargo was tense, and his senses were heightened to an even greater level of awareness. His ears picked up other sounds—a faint rustling of brush, a whispered word that he couldn't make out, the scrape of boot leather on the ground. Men were sneaking up on the clearing.

One of them walked right past him.

The man never noticed Fargo standing there in the shadows. As he moved between the Trailsman and the fire, Fargo got a good look at him. He was young and fairly well dressed, with a handsome but cruel face. He had a gun in his hand and looked eager to use it.

Fargo struck swiftly and silently. He drove the metal buttplate of the Henry against the back of the man's neck. It was possible to kill an hombre by hitting him like that. Fargo didn't want this skulker dead, so he held back a little on the blow, striking just hard enough to make the man pitch to the ground, out cold.

He made a little noise when he fell. Fargo hoped that wouldn't be enough to panic the man's companions. No shots rang out, so maybe they hadn't heard the slight commotion. Fargo slid through the darkness, hoping to run into another of the lurkers.

A moment later, he did so. The dark shape loomed up to his right and leaned toward him. A voice hissed, "Donnegan? That you?"

"Nope," Fargo said. With his right hand he rammed the muzzle of the rifle into the man's belly as hard as he could.

At the same time, his left hand closed around the man's throat, choking off any cry of pain or warning. The muscles in Fargo's arm and shoulder bunched under the buckskin as he forced the man to the ground.

With his breath knocked out of him and Fargo's iron fingers clamped around his throat to prevent any air from getting in, the man was too weak and stunned to put up a fight. In a minute or so, he went limp as consciousness left him.

Fargo straightened. He didn't know how many men were sneaking up on the camp, but he had taken two of them out of the fight. He continued circling the clearing, looking for more enemies.

They were ready to make their move, however. Two men holding revolvers stepped into the circle of light cast by the fire. Leveling the weapons at the wagon, one of them yelled, "Come outta there, you damn Haddons!"

Fargo was part of the way around the clearing, to the right of the men. A quick step brought him into the light as well. As he saw the barrel of Bodie's rifle thrust out from under the wagon, he shouted, "Stay inside!" and hoped that Junie and Calvin and the other youngsters would heed the command.

He snapped the Henry to his shoulder as the two men whirled toward him, startled by his shout.

"Drop the guns!" Fargo called to them.

He saw instantly that they weren't going to. The barrels had dropped a little due to the surprise the men experienced when Fargo challenged them, but now resolve appeared on their snarling faces and they jerked the pistols up to fire.

Under the circumstances, Fargo wasn't going to give them the first shot, and neither was Bodie. Smoke plumed from the barrel of the old man's rifle as he fired. A split second later, Fargo's Henry cracked.

One of the men was struck cleanly in the chest and knocked off his feet. The other one was hit but managed to stay upright. Flame spurted from the muzzle of his gun. Fargo heard the wind rip of the slug as it passed close by his ear.

He was already levering another round into the Henry's chamber. He triggered the second shot and saw the man spin around as the bullet bored a clean hole through his right arm. His revolver flew out of his hands.

Fargo lunged forward and swung the Henry. The stock smashed into the man's solar plexus and doubled him over. A swift kick from Fargo knocked his legs out from under him and toppled him to the ground.

Fargo brought his right foot down on the man's shoulder, pinning him where he was. The muzzle of Fargo's rifle dug painfully into his neck, just under his chin.

"How many of you are there?" Fargo demanded.

The man was in pain from his two wounds, and he couldn't talk very well with the rifle barrel prodding his throat. But he managed to grate out, "Go to hell!"

"You'll be there before me, because I'm going to

blow your head off in about another two seconds! Now, tell me how many men were with you."

The man must have seen the menace in Fargo's face and heard it in his voice. He gasped, "D-don't shoot! There—there were three men with me!"

"Four of you in all?"

"Y-yeah. That's right."

Fargo nodded. He thought the man was too scared not to be telling the truth. One man was down, evidently dead or badly wounded, two were lying in the woods, knocked out, and this one had a couple of bullet holes in him. They were all accounted for.

"Who are you?" Fargo asked. The man had thinning brown hair and a beard. He didn't match the descriptions Junie had given him of Garrett or Joel Braxton.

"M-my name is Lawrence D-Donnegan," the man gasped. "Please, mister. I'm shot and h-hurtin' awful bad."

In addition to the wound in his right arm, Donnegan had been hit in the right leg, too, although that wound wasn't bleeding much and was probably just a graze.

Fargo couldn't muster up much sympathy. He asked, "Are you related to the Braxtons?"

"Hugo's my c-cousin."

"Did he send you after the Haddon youngsters?"

"He sent . . . his boys. Please, mister—"

"The sooner you tell me all about it," Fargo said, "the sooner I'll let you up and those wounds will be tended to. You can talk, or you can lay there and bleed to death."

"I—I'll talk!"

Fargo looked at Bodie, who had crawled out from under the wagon after reloading his rifle. "Is that one dead?" he asked, jerking his head toward the other man who had been shot.

Bodie prodded the man with his foot. The man's head lolled back and forth loosely.

"Deader'n hell," Bodie announced, a note of satisfaction in his voice.

"There are two more out in the woods." Fargo held the Henry with one hand and pointed with the other. "I knocked them out, but they may be stirring around by now. Take Calvin and Luke with you, tie them up, and drag them in where we can keep an eye on them."

"Durned tootin'," Bodie agreed with a nod. He motioned to the wagon, where the youngsters were now looking out, wide-eyed, scared by the shooting but still calm. "Come on, boys."

Calvin and Luke scrambled out of the wagon and joined Bodie. Fargo noticed that Calvin was wearing the gun belt. He hoped the boy wouldn't get trigger-happy.

Turning his attention back to the man at his feet, Fargo said, "All right. You were going to tell me what you're doing here."

"Yeah. It—it was like this. . . ."

Black Hugo Braxton was famous for his rages. He could curse and rant with the best—or the worst—of them, and he had been known to get so mad that he hauled out the hogleg at his waist and started blazing away wildly. Everybody in the family knew to stay out of his way when he got like that.

But when he was quiet, as he was now, he was even more frightening.

His dark eyes burned intensely, as if they held the banked fires of hell itself, as he said to his sons, "You did what?"

"Took care of that Haddon problem for you, Pa," Garrett replied, a note of pride in his voice. Maybe he hadn't noticed how angry his father looked. Larry

Donnegan had noticed, though, and he thought his second cousin Garrett was a damned fool.

The Braxton house was big, dark, and hulking. Hugo leaned back in the heavy chair in his study and faced the four men in front of the desk—Garrett, Joel, Donnegan, and a nephew named Seth Colbert. All four of them had been at the Haddon place a few days earlier, along with several other friends and relatives of the Braxton family, when Walter Haddon and his sharecropper friends had been strung up.

From there they had ridden on over to Sedalia, to a whorehouse Garrett and Joel frequently patronized, for a few days of drinking and cavorting with the soiled doves who worked there. Lynching a man, even a Haddon, left sort of a bad taste in a fella's mouth, and the best way to get rid of it was with a spell of debauchery.

Finally, when they had run low on money, they left the place with pounding headaches, fuzzy mouths, and a feeling of having been drained of all their vital juices as well as their funds. Mounting up, they rode back to Braxton's Lick, the rest veering off to head for their homes, while Donnegan and Colbert had accompanied Garrett and Joel to the Braxton homestead. Garrett claimed to have a jug stashed there, and a little hair of the dog was just what they needed.

But Black Hugo had confronted them angrily when they got there, calling them into his study. "I hear that somethin' happened over at the Haddon place the other night," he'd said as he sat down behind the desk.

That was when Garrett and Joel had grinned at each other and Garrett had said, "You don't have to worry about Haddon anymore, Pa. We handled that for you, didn't we, little brother?" He nudged Joel with his elbow, and they both laughed.

Hugo had gotten quiet and mean looking and demanded to know what they were talking about. Garrett had repeated his boast, and now Donnegan was waiting to see what was going to happen.

He figured Hugo was due to erupt any minute, just like the top blowing off a volcano.

"I hear that Haddon, Tompkins, Curry, and Donner got themselves hanged," Hugo said, still holding it in somehow, to Donnegan's amazement.

"Yeah," Joel said. He laughed and added, "You should've been there. It was funny as hell the way they kicked and jerked and messed their pants while they was stranglin' to death. I never seen anything quite so funny."

"Sheriff Reynolds went along with that?"

Garrett said, "He knew he didn't have any choice in the matter. Cousin Oliver's not stupid."

Reynolds wasn't really their cousin, but they called him that anyway. And it was true that he wasn't stupid enough to oppose what he thought were Black Hugo's wishes.

But as Donnegan looked at the old man behind the desk, a bad feeling began to grow inside him. He wondered just how much Hugo had known beforehand about what was going to happen.

Not much, as quickly became apparent when Hugo said to his sons, "So you just took it upon yourselves to lynch Haddon and his friends?"

"He had it comin', Pa," Garrett said. "You made him a fair offer, and he should've agreed to sell out to you. When he didn't, he was just askin' for trouble."

"Hangin' a man's illegal," Hugo pointed out.

Garrett waved a hand. "Don't worry about that. We made sure it looked like Haddon stole some of our cows. That gave us an excuse to go to the sheriff and tell him you wanted to swear out a warrant. Then Haddon and his bunch resisted arrest—or at least that's the story Cousin Oliver will tell everybody. Nobody's gonna think twice about those no-accounts gettin' strung up, Pa."

Hugo's eyes narrowed. "You had *my* name put on the warrant."

"Well . . . yeah." For the first time, Garrett began to look a little nervous. Joel fidgeted beside him.

"All because you heard me bitchin' about Haddon and took it on yourselves to do something about it."

"That's right." Garrett summoned up a bit of defiance as he lifted his chin and went on, "You're all the time tellin' Joel and me we got to start thinkin' for ourselves. Well, now that we did, you act like we done somethin' wrong."

Hugo put his hands flat on the desk and pushed himself upright. "I told you you need to *think* for yourselves! What kind of thinkin' is it for you to get me mixed up in a lynchin'?"

"Don't worry about it, Pa," Joel said. "Nobody's gonna talk. It was just friends and family there—"

"And the sheriff and two of his deputies!" Hugo snorted.

"Reynolds is one of us," Garrett said. "And his deputies take his orders. They won't say anything."

"Maybe not, but there was somebody else there you're forgettin'."

Garrett frowned. "Who?"

Hugo leaned forward, his hands still resting on the desk, and bared his yellow teeth in a snarl. "Those Haddon brats! You let them live, didn't you?"

"Well, yeah," Garrett said nervously. "They're just kids. We didn't figure even Cousin Oliver would stand still for them bein' hurt, especially since they didn't do anything to fight us."

"So you let 'em go?"

"We made 'em get off the place. When we rode by

there on the way home a while ago, it was empty. Deserted. Won't nobody stand in your way when you claim it, Pa."

"What happened to the young'uns?"

Garrett shrugged. "I think they were plannin' to go down to Springfield. There's Haddon kin down there."

"How were they gonna get there?"

"Shank's mare," Garrett said. "We wouldn't let them take the wagon or the mules. All that'll belong to you once you take the place over."

In that soft, scary voice, Black Hugo said, "You reckon those kids won't tell folks what happened when they get to Springfield?"

"Who's gonna believe 'em?" Garrett asked. "They're just kids."

"Maybe so, but that's one hell of a story they've got to tell. And we don't have near as many friends in Springfield as we do up here around Braxton's Lick. Could be somebody might listen to 'em. They might even try to get a federal marshal to come up here and start pokin' around."

"Cousin Oliver will back us up—"

"Oliver Reynolds will mess *his* britches the first time a federal lawman says howdy-do to him!" Black Hugo was roaring at last, and Donnegan was almost relieved by the explosion. He hadn't cared for the waiting.

"Pa, listen—" Garrett began.

"No, you listen to me! Reynolds will talk, and so will them deputies of his! The only way to stop it is to make sure nobody ever comes up here to investigate what happened to Haddon."

Joel said, "You're sayin' we shouldn't have let those kids go?"

Hugo slammed a fist down on the desk. "I'm sayin' you got to go after them, find them, and *kill them*!"

A stunned silence fell over the room. Both Garrett and Joel opened and closed their mouths, but no words came out.

It was Seth Colbert who finally spoke up. "I don't know if we can kill some kids, Uncle Hugo. That's liable to cause some real trouble."

Hugo sneered. "Worse than hangin' for what you did to Haddon and his friends?"

"I still say nobody's gonna care about that," Garrett said stubbornly.

"You can't count on that. The safety of this family comes first, and the only way we can be sure of bein' safe is if those little Haddons are dead. You're so damned quick to jump in and take it on yourselves to do things. Well, go and take care of the mess you made!"

"I don't know . . ." Joel said. "Seems mighty risky to me."

Garrett rubbed at his jaw in thought. "Maybe not," he said. "Those young'uns were goin' to walk down to Springfield. They ain't had time to get there yet. We ought to be able to catch up to them in a day or two on horseback. There are lots of woods between here and there. If we were to grab 'em, take 'em out in the forest, kill them and dump their bodies in a ravine somewhere or one of those lakes that're so deep . . . nobody would ever know what happened to them."

"I dunno if I can kill a kid," Seth said.

Black Hugo drew the huge, heavy, old cap-and-ball pistol at his waist and pointed it at Seth, earing back the hammer as he did so. "You were part of it," he said with a murderous glare. "You can go along and help, or I'll shoot you where you stand."

Seth paled, swallowed hard, and drew back a step. "Don't shoot, Uncle Hugo," he said in a shaky voice.

"I was just sayin' . . . but never mind about that. I'll go along. You can count on me, sir."

"Damn well better be able to, or I'll hunt you down and shoot you like the dog you are." Hugo switched his fiery gaze to Donnegan. "What about you, Larry?"

"I'll do whatever you say, Hugo," Donnegan replied. "You know that."

Hugo nodded curtly. "Good. Round up the other fellas who were with you and take them along, too. If the eight of you can't find and kill those kids . . . well, in that case, just don't bother to come back. Because if you fail me, I'll shoot you on sight."

None of them doubted for a second that Black Hugo Braxton meant what he said.

Fargo listened to the story with growing horror. It was hard to believe that anyone could be as cold-blooded and vicious as Donnegan described Black Hugo Braxton being.

And yet he believed the man's story. Donnegan's pained, halting words had the ring of truth. Braxton had sent Donnegan and the others out to murder the seven Haddon youngsters.

Without relieving the pressure on the rifle barrel pressed to Donnegan's throat, Fargo asked, "You said there were eight of you. Where are the other four?"

"We—we split up a couple of days ago," Donnegan said. "There's more than one road . . . that goes to Springfield. Garrett and Joel . . . and a couple of the boys . . . took another trail."

Fargo nodded. "Who's this with you?"

"The one you shot . . . is Seth. The other two are just . . . friends of the family. Warren Rogers and . . . Andrew Pine."

"They're lucky they're not dead, too." The two men had been dragged into camp by Bodie, Calvin, and

Luke while Donnegan was telling his story. Their hands were tied behind their backs with their own belts. They had regained consciousness but hadn't said anything yet as they lay beside the wagon, staring around in a mixture of anger and fear for their lives.

"Please, mister—" Donnegan said.

"I'm not through with you yet," Fargo snapped. "You know the settlement of Bear Creek?"

"Yeah . . . We came through there . . . earlier today."

"Did something happen there?" Fargo asked tautly.

Donnegan licked his lips, and Fargo could tell that he didn't want to answer. But as Fargo increased the pressure a little on the rifle barrel, Donnegan said hurriedly, "We stopped there!"

"Why?"

"To—to ask if anybody had seen those kids."

"And what happened?"

"There was . . . a woman at the roadhouse. She said she never—never saw anybody like that come through Bear Creek."

Lizbeth must have realized that the four riders meant harm to the youngsters, so she had lied. Fargo wasn't surprised.

"Seth, though . . . he got it in his head the woman was lyin'. He started . . . slappin' her around."

Fargo's finger tightened slightly on the Henry's trigger. Not enough to make the rifle go off, but enough so that he had to force himself to relax it.

Donnegan must have seen that, because he started talking even faster. "I didn't touch her myself. I swear I didn't. This fella came out of the roadhouse. . . . He looked like he'd been hurt somehow. He was bandaged up . . . and cussed Seth and tried to fight him, but Seth walloped him over the head with a pistol and told the woman he'd beat the fella's brains out if she didn't tell us the truth . . . so then she said she had seen that bunch of kids, that they just left there this mornin' in a wagon . . . We knew then that we could catch up to you."

"I saw smoke late this afternoon," Fargo said. "Did you have anything to do with that?"

"Seth was mad . . . 'cause the woman had lied to us, so he . . . he burned down that roadhouse."

"Was anybody hurt, or caught in the fire?"

"The man and the woman . . . well, Seth pistol-whipped 'em pretty bad. But they wasn't killed, I swear it! And nobody was in the roadhouse when it burned down. I swear that, too, mister."

Bodie was standing to the side, listening to the story. He turned his head and spat on Seth Colbert's corpse. "Mangy damned polecat," he said.

Fargo wasn't completely convinced that Seth had been to blame for everything that had happened—Donnegan could have colored the story so as to make himself look not quite so bad—but since he hadn't been there, he couldn't prove otherwise.

And despite his hard-nosed attitude, he wasn't going to kill anybody in cold blood, either, even if maybe they deserved it.

"You'd better be telling me the truth about not killing anybody in Bear Creek," he said to Donnegan. "If I find out different later on, I'll be seeing you again."

"It's the truth, mister, I swear it!" Donnegan let out a groan. "I've told you everything I know. Now will you do something about my arm and my leg?"

Fargo stepped back and took the rifle away from Donnegan's throat. "Bodie, how are you at patching up bullet holes?"

"Fair to middlin'," the old-timer said. "I'm sorta rough about it, though. Ain't nobody ever accused me o' bein' gentle."

"See what you can do for Donnegan." Fargo smiled thinly. "I don't reckon you have to worry about being too rough, though. I don't think he's going to complain."

7

While Bodie tended to Donnegan's injuries, Fargo went over to the wagon and said to the children, "I reckon you heard all of that."

Junie nodded. She looked as pale as she had the day before when Fargo first met the youngsters.

"Black Hugo wants us dead," she said. "Somehow, that doesn't surprise me."

"Me, either," Fargo agreed. "I worried about that as soon as I heard about what happened to your father."

"What are we gonna do?" Calvin asked.

"You're going on to Springfield like you planned," Fargo said.

"But you heard him! They're after us!"

Fargo nodded. "Yes, but Garrett and Joel are on the wrong trail. If we can get you down there before they catch up, they won't be able to do anything to you there in the middle of town."

"Do you think we should talk to the law, like Hugo's worried about?" Junie asked. "I'll tell you the truth, Skye, I never even thought about that. I'm just so used to everybody knuckling under to the Braxtons, it didn't occur to me that it might be different somewhere else."

"We'll figure that out when the time comes," Fargo promised her. "For now we just need to worry about getting you there."

Donnegan let out a howl of pain as Bodie cleaned his wounds with whiskey from a flask the old-timer dug out from under his bearskin coat. "Don't carry on so," Bodie snapped. "You'd really have somethin' to holler about if you let them bullet holes fester."

He took out a bowie knife and used it to cut strips off the tail of Donnegan's shirt, then bound those strips around the man's arm and leg as crude bandages. Straightening from the task, Bodie looked at Fargo and nodded.

"Reckon that's the best I can do. He won't die from them wounds, more's the pity."

"Put him with the others and tie him up, too," Fargo said. "Calvin, Luke, give Mr. Strickland a hand."

Soon all three of the prisoners sat next to the wagon, propped up against a rear wheel.

"Might as well climb back inside and get some more sleep," Fargo told the children. "These three won't bother you anymore."

"What about Seth?" Donnegan asked. "It ain't proper to just leave him layin' out like that."

"You're right," Fargo said. "We'll cover him up with a blanket and bury him in the morning."

Donnegan looked a little surprised, but he nodded and said, "All right. Thanks."

"Any consideration is more than the likes of you deserve," Fargo said coldly. "I'd bury even a rabid dog, though, if I had to kill it."

He got a blanket from the wagon and spread it over the bloody corpse. He did it as much for the children as anything. They didn't need to be looking at that.

Bodie came over to Fargo and said, "I'm wide awake now. Why don't you go crawl under the wagon and get some shut-eye, whilst you've got the chance?"

Fargo thought it over and nodded. "That's probably a good idea. The others who are after the kids probably aren't anywhere around here, so there shouldn't be any more trouble tonight. We'll keep our guard up, though. If you start to get sleepy, wake me up and I'll take over."

Bodie nodded and said, "Durned tootin'."

Fargo wrapped himself in his bedroll and fell asleep quickly. It was a deep, dreamless slumber—for a while, anyway. Then his sleep began to be haunted by the images Junie had told him about the night before: the burning barn, the four men dangling and swaying on the hang ropes, the cruel, laughing faces of Garrett and Joel Braxton. . . .

Those dreams were mixed with others about Black Hugo Braxton and the way he had ruthlessly set his sons and the other men on the trail of the surviving Haddons.

Once the children were safe in Springfield, Fargo would head north again, bound for Braxton's Lick to see to it that justice was dealt out to Black Hugo. According to Donnegan's story, Hugo hadn't known in advance about the planned lynching of Walter Haddon and the sharecroppers.

But it was Black Hugo who had issued the orders for the murder of seven innocent youngsters, and the man had to answer for that. Fargo would work within the law to bring that about, if he could.

If he couldn't . . . Well, this was the frontier, after all. There was such a thing as rough justice, and sometimes that was the only thing that worked.

Skye Fargo was no back shooter, no dry-gulcher. But he knew that if he stood up to Hugo Braxton,

Hugo would come after him. Then it would be every man for himself, and devil take the hindmost.

From everything Fargo had heard, Black Hugo was a pretty close cousin to Satan himself. . . .

Fargo came awake with a start. Pale gray light filled the clearing. Dawn wasn't far off. It was as cold as Fargo had expected it to be. The air was so frigid it seemed to grab at his lungs as he breathed it in.

He was about to crawl out from under the wagon when he heard a sudden rush of footsteps, the thud of a fist against flesh and bone, and the harsh breathing of a struggle.

Fargo slung his blankets aside and rolled out quickly, his hand going to the butt of his gun as he did so. He came up on one knee, his eyes searching the dimly lit clearing for the source of the sounds he'd heard.

"Drop it, mister!" a man shouted.

Fargo turned to his left and saw one of the prisoners—he had no idea if it was Warren Rogers or Andrew Pine—pointing a gun at him. The man's other hand was locked around the throat of Calvin Haddon, who struggled futilely against the cruel grip.

"Drop it!" the man ordered again.

Surrender went against the grain for Fargo. But the man had the drop on him. Fargo couldn't turn and fire before the man put a bullet in him.

Besides that, Calvin was starting to turn blue, and his struggles were weakening. Another minute or so and he would choke to death.

"All right," Fargo said, lowering his Colt. "I'll put the gun down. But turn the boy loose."

"Drop the gun first!"

Fargo set the Colt on the ground in front of him. He could still snatch it up and bring it into play in a hurry, if he got the chance.

The man flung Calvin to the ground. The boy landed hard and lay there gasping for air and writhing feebly. He had come close to passing out and dying.

The gun in the man's hand was Calvin's Colt Navy, Fargo realized. He didn't know how the prisoner had gotten loose or how he got his hands on Calvin's gun, but that didn't matter now.

Bodie came hurrying out of the trees but stopped short as he saw the man pointing the gun at Fargo. He started to lift his rifle, but the former prisoner said, "I'll kill him if you try it, old man!"

"Shoot him, Warren!" Donnegan urged from the ground where he still sat beside the wagon wheel. "Kill Fargo while you've got the chance!"

Fargo was tensed and ready to throw himself to the side in a desperate attempt to avoid the bullet if Warren Rogers fired, but Rogers held off.

"Not yet," he said. "We can use him." To Bodie, he said, "Put your rifle down and turn my friends loose."

Bodie looked at the Trailsman. "Fargo . . . ?"

"Better do what he says," Fargo told him. "He's got the upper hand . . . for now, anyway."

Rogers grinned. "Damn right I've got the upper hand. I'm gonna go back to Black Hugo and tell him that not only did I get rid of those kids, I killed the famous Skye Fargo, too."

So they knew who he was. It wouldn't have been hard for them to overhear his name the night before, when he was talking to Bodie and the Haddon youngsters. Clearly they had heard of him.

"That won't win you any favors from Braxton," Fargo pointed out. "He doesn't know me from Adam."

"He'll be grateful, though, when he hears about how you helped those little bastards. He'll figure you deserved to die for that."

Fargo heard people moving around inside the wagon.

The commotion had roused Junie and the children from their sleep. He said sharply, "Junie, you and the others stay in there."

"That won't do any good, Fargo," Rogers said. "That canvas cover won't protect them."

Bodie finished untying Donnegan and Pine. He stepped back, his weathered face tight with anger. Donnegan grabbed hold of the wheel and pulled himself up. Then he swung a vicious, unexpected backhand that cracked across Bodie's face and sent the old man tumbling backward off his feet.

Bodie sat up and rubbed his jaw. "Fine thanks I get for seein' to it that you didn't bleed to death," he grumbled.

"Shut up, old man," Donnegan said. To Pine, he went on. "I saw them put our guns under the wagon last night. Get 'em."

Pine crawled under the wagon to recover the guns while Bodie looked over at Fargo and said, "Sorry, son. I stepped into the trees to answer the call o' nature. That can take a damn long time when you get to be my age. Reckon that skunk got loose whilst I was gone."

Rogers chuckled. "I'd been working at that belt around my wrists all night. Lost some hide getting it loose, but I reckon it was worth it. Then that kid climbed out of the wagon and walked right by me, with the gun sticking up from his holster. Damn fool."

Calvin had gotten his breath back enough so that he was sitting up again. He looked miserable, as if he thought that the whole thing was his fault. While it was true that he should have been more careful and shouldn't have gotten so close to the prisoners, Fargo didn't blame him for everything.

"He never expected me to grab him," Rogers went on. "He'll pay for being careless."

"You don't want to do this," Fargo said. "You can't be a low enough snake to murder children."

"Kids die all the time," Rogers shot back with a sneer. "Better them than me and my friends. Because that's what's liable to happen if we go back to Black Hugo and tell him that we failed."

Rogers might be right about that, given everything Fargo had heard about Black Hugo Braxton.

Pine came out from under the wagon with the revolvers Fargo had taken from the men the night before. He gave one of them to Donnegan and kept a couple for himself, since Rogers had Calvin's Colt Navy. Donnegan limped around to the front of the wagon, keeping his distance from the vehicle, and pointed his gun at the opening behind the driver's seat.

"You kids come on out of there," he ordered.

Junie climbed out first, wrapped in a blanket. She stepped down awkwardly to the ground, looking pale and frightened. Fargo's jaw clenched in anger and frustration.

"Mister," Junie said tentatively, "mister, isn't there anything we can do to change your mind?" She moved closer to Donnegan. "Maybe something *I* can do?"

A leering grin spread over the man's face as he lowered his gun a little. "Maybe I'll think about it, sis," he said. "Why don't you try to convince me? You never know, it might work."

"How about this?" Junie said. She took another step closer to Donnegan, lifted the carbine from the folds of the blanket that enveloped her, and shot him in the chest at close range.

Fargo saw the flame lance out from the carbine's barrel and touch Donnegan's coat. The bullet drove the man backward.

At the same instant, Fargo dived forward and rolled

over, snatching his Colt from the ground as he did so. Rogers fired instinctively, but the slug sizzled through the air where Fargo had been a split second earlier.

Then Fargo was stretched out on his belly, thumbing off shots as fast as he could. The bullets plowed into Rogers at an upward angle and lifted him off his feet, throwing him back against the wagon. Blood fountained from his throat as the last of Fargo's shots tore through it.

Pine had a gun in each hand but didn't get a chance to use the weapons. Bodie lunged at him from where the old-timer lay on the ground. He hit Pine's legs and knocked him off balance. As Pine staggered, Bodie brought up his bowie knife and buried the razor-sharp blade in Pine's groin. Pine screamed, dropped the guns, and collapsed as Bodie ripped the knife free and blood spurted from the wound.

Bodie was on top of the man in a flash, the knife rising and falling. A thick coating of crimson clung to the blade as the old-timer drove it in and out of Pine's chest. Pine's arms were flung out to his sides. He arched and flopped and gave a long, bubbling scream before he fell back, dead.

"That's enough, Bodie," Fargo said sharply as he got to his feet. "He's done for."

Fargo turned quickly toward Junie and Donnegan. Donnegan lay on his back, his eyes wide open, his mouth working. He still held the gun in his hand. As he tried to lift it, Fargo stepped closer and kicked it away. He pointed his Colt at Donnegan, but then the man sighed and the life went out of his eyes.

Junie stood there, trembling a little. She clutched the carbine tightly. "I shot him," she said. "I figured he didn't know I had a rifle, so I got as close as I could and I shot him."

"And it's a good thing you did, too," Fargo said as

he gently took the weapon out of her hands. "If you hadn't, there's a good chance all of us would have wound up dead, all the way down to little Arlo."

"I never killed a man before. But . . . he was there. He was there that night."

Fargo didn't have to ask her what night she was talking about. He knew that Donnegan had been one of the men who'd lynched Walter Haddon.

Junie drew a deep breath and turned to Fargo. "He had it coming," she said, and from the look in her eyes, he knew she would be all right. Ending a man's life was a heavy responsibility for anyone, but knowing that the death was justified made the burden bearable.

Calvin picked up the gun Rogers had dropped and put it back in its holster. "I'm sorry, Mr. Fargo," he said. "I didn't know he'd gotten his hands loose."

"Never get close enough for a prisoner to grab you," Fargo advised. "And always assume the worst is possible . . . because it usually is."

Calvin nodded solemnly. "I'll remember."

Fargo thought the youngster *would* remember. Calvin was stubborn, argumentative, and full of the arrogance of youth. But he wasn't stupid, and he could learn from his mistakes.

They had four dead men on their hands now. While Junie and the younger children built up the fire and started preparing breakfast, Fargo, Bodie, Calvin, and Luke dragged the corpses into the woods and set about digging a mass grave. Fargo had bought a shovel at Merriman's, so the two men and the boys took turns digging until they had a hole big enough for all four bodies.

By the time that grim chore was completed, breakfast was ready. Sitting around a warm campfire, eating bacon and hotcakes, washing the food down with hot coffee—those things took away the lingering thoughts of blood and death and made everyone feel human again.

When they were finished with breakfast, Calvin and Luke hitched up the team while Fargo and Bodie got the horses and Bodie's mule ready to ride. They found the mounts that Donnegan and the other men had ridden, but not wanting to take them along, Fargo stripped the saddles and bridles from them and turned the animals loose. Some farmer in the area would wind up with an unexpected bounty.

Less than an hour after the sun rose, the wagon was rolling down the road to Springfield, with Fargo and Calvin riding out front. Today, though, Bodie and Luke hung back to keep an eye on the trail behind them. Despite his age, Bodie's senses were keen, and if he became aware of any signs of trouble approaching them, he would send Luke galloping ahead to warn the others.

The day passed without any problems, however. Fargo had worried that Garrett, Joel, and the other searchers might be close enough to have heard the flurry of gunshots that morning, but evidently that hadn't been the case.

He and Bodie took turns standing guard again that night. This time nothing happened except that the children got a good night's sleep.

Two more days and nights passed without any sign of Garrett and Joel. The temptation was to relax and let their guard down a little, but Fargo knew better than to allow that to happen. The children were still in danger and would be until they reached Springfield. Even then, it wasn't beyond the realm of possibility that the men who wanted to kill them might make an attempt on their lives.

As for the youngsters themselves, the passage of time, even a few days, was enough to dull some of the

117

bad memories. They enjoyed traveling in the wagon, and a lot of talk and laughter came from the vehicle.

They had never been to Springfield before. Some of them had never been more than a few miles from the farm outside Braxton's Lick. This was all new to them, and they were excited.

At night, the feeling of camaraderie continued around the campfire. Fargo looked at and listened to the Haddon children, and he knew that they would be able to cope and make lives for themselves, especially if they weren't split up.

Fargo thought about Lizbeth and Grundy, too, and hoped that they hadn't been hurt too bad. Since he'd be going north anyway, once he got the kids to safety, he planned to stop at the settlement of Bear Creek and see how they were doing. He had wanted to ride back up there when he heard Donnegan's story, but he knew his first responsibility lay with the youngsters.

They had been making good time, and by the fifth day Fargo knew they had covered well over half the distance to Springfield. They might reach the city the next day. He felt an urgency driving him, and that feeling must have communicated itself to the others.

Fargo was ready to get there, and so was everybody else.

There were more farms around now, and that night they stopped at one owned by a family named Forrest. The farmer was glad to let them park the wagon in front of the rambling plank house that his family called home. Mrs. Forrest insisted that they all come in for a home-cooked meal.

That sounded good to Fargo, and it did to the others, too. The Forrests had four children between the ages of five and twelve, and those youngsters were glad to have someone else around to play with, even if it was only for one night.

After supper, Fargo, Bodie, and Howard Forrest sat outside in cane-bottomed chairs. Bodie and Forrest filled and lit pipes. The weather had warmed up considerably, although the night air still held a slight chill. There hadn't been any more rain or sleet.

Forrest puffed on his pipe for a few minutes in silence, then said, "I ain't meanin' to pry, Mr. Fargo, but I got a feelin' that there's more to this than you've told me. What happened to the parents of those children?"

"You're right," Fargo admitted. "And I should have told you that by helping us, you may be letting yourself in for some trouble."

Forrest's rough-hewn, weather-beaten face hardened in the light that came from inside the house. "Is my family in danger?"

"Probably not. But there are some men who are after those kids. Their father was lynched a couple of weeks ago, and the varmints responsible for that want to make sure nobody ever tells the law what really happened."

Forrest clamped his teeth down hard on the stem of his old corncob pipe. "I appreciate you bein' honest with me."

Bodie asked the farmer, "Would you have turned us away if you'd knowed the whole story?"

"Turn away children who have been on the road for a week?" Forrest shook his head. "No, my wife never would've allowed that. But this way we'll know to be on the lookout for trouble after you're gone."

"That's already happened once," Fargo said bluntly. "Some folks up north of here, in a place called Bear Creek, got hurt and their place was burned down."

Forrest bristled. "Anybody comes around here lookin' to cause trouble, I'll dust the seat o' their pants with buckshot."

"Don't underestimate them," Fargo warned. "They're killers."

"I was in the Mexican War," Forrest said proudly. "Went up Chapultepec with old Winfield Scott and kicked the Mexicans right off that hill. I can handle a few troublemaking varmints."

Fargo hoped the man was right. Even more so, he hoped that Forrest never had to find out whether or not he could handle the Braxtons and their friends.

The Haddon wagon was back on the road early the next morning. Fargo hoped to reach Springfield by nightfall. The youngsters were just as eager, even though they had enjoyed the visit with the Forrest family.

They stopped at midday where a creek ran next to the road for a short distance. Mrs. Forrest had packed some sandwiches for them, slices of roast beef between thick slabs of bread, so they didn't have to prepare a meal.

It was only when they gathered around to eat that they realized Jonas was gone.

Junie cried out in surprise and fear. She ran a few steps back up the road and called, "Jonas! Jonas, where are you?" before Fargo caught up to her and put a hand on her arm.

"Take it easy," he told her. "We'll find him. He probably just wandered off to look at something in the woods."

Arlo surprised them by speaking up. "That's right. I seen him."

Fargo turned toward the smallest and youngest of the Haddons. "What did you see, Arlo?" he asked. "Which way did Jonas go?"

Arlo pointed. "He was over by the creek, right after we stopped. A deer came up on the other side to get a drink, and Jonas chased him."

Junie asked, "How did he get across the creek?"

"On them rocks." Arlo pointed again.

Even though Fargo hadn't witnessed the incident, he could see in his mind's eye how it happened. There were several good-sized rocks in the creek bed, and it would have been easy enough for an agile boy to jump from one to the other until he was on the far side of the creek.

Surely Jonas had known that he couldn't catch a deer, but he must have wanted a closer look at this one. The woods on the other side of the stream were pretty thick. The deer had bounded off, and Jonas had gone after it, disappearing into the trees. That had to be the way it happened.

Then, it was possible that Jonas had gotten turned around and hadn't been able to find his way back to the wagon. Fargo was confident, though, that he could track the boy down.

"I'll go get him," he said to Junie. "Don't worry."

Calvin said, "Can I come with you, Mr. Fargo?"

After a moment's consideration, Fargo nodded. "I think that'll be all right. Bodie, keep an eye on things here."

The old-timer nodded and gave his usual "Durned tootin' " agreement.

Fargo and Calvin stepped from rock to rock across the stream. Once they were on the other side they plunged into the woods, with Fargo in the lead. Already, he had spotted the tracks left behind by the deer and some small, telltale signs of Jonas's pursuit of it. He didn't think it would take them too long to catch up to the boy.

"I ain't had my target practice today," Calvin pointed out. At least once every day while they had been on the road, Fargo had let him fire a few rounds from the Colt Navy. Calvin could draw the gun fairly quickly now without nearly dropping it, and he hit what he aimed at more often than not.

"That'll have to wait," Fargo told him. "You can't go shooting blindly out in the woods like this. A bullet can carry quite a distance, and you never know what you might hit. Your little brother's out here somewhere, you know."

"Yeah, that's true," Calvin admitted. "I hadn't thought about that."

"You have to think if you're going to use a gun. That's one of the most important parts of it, knowing when to shoot and when not to."

Calvin nodded. "I'll remember that."

They moved deeper into the woods, Fargo watching for the branches that had been bent back, the rocks that had been kicked over, and the occasional track left behind by Jonas. He was about to call out the boy's name when he heard something that made him stop suddenly and lift a hand to motion Calvin to a halt as well.

Fargo heard somebody sobbing.

The sound came from somewhere close by. The Trailsman's ears led him unerringly to the source. Carefully, he cat-footed through the brush, revolver in hand now. Calvin followed behind him, wide-eyed with a mixture of fear and anticipation. Fargo glanced back, saw Calvin reaching for the Colt Navy, and with a curt shake of his head signaled for the youngster to leave the gun in its holster for now, until they were sure of what was going on.

Fargo's main worry was that somehow the Braxtons had caught up to them and grabbed Jonas, but there was also the possibility that the boy had hurt himself some way. A lot of things could happen out here in the woods, and most of them were bad.

They came to a small rocky knob that thrust up out

of the ground. The sobs came from the other side of it. Fargo eased around the knob, gun leveled and ready for use.

He stopped and felt his tense muscles relax. Jonas was sitting at the base of a small pine tree, his back against the trunk. He was alone, and he looked to be all right.

"Jonas," Fargo said quietly, not wanting to spook the boy any more than he had to.

Jonas shot to his feet, turning quickly toward Fargo and Calvin. His tear-streaked face was pale.

"Calvin!" he cried out. He ran past Fargo and threw his arms around his older brother. "Calvin, I got lost! I—I was so scared I'd never find my way back!"

Calvin patted Jonas awkwardly on the back and said, "It's all right. You're safe now. Mr. Fargo and I won't let anything happen to you."

Fargo put a hand on Jonas' shoulder. "You're not hurt, are you?"

"N-no." Jonas sniffled and wiped the back of his hand across his nose. "I saw a deer, and it was so pretty I wanted to get a b-better look at it. Then when I got out here in the woods, I—I got turned around and didn't know which way to go."

His sniffles got stronger, and Fargo figured he was about to start sobbing again. But Calvin said, "You're fine now, so stop crying, Jonas."

"You—you're not mad at me?"

"You don't need to wander off like that," Fargo said. "But there was no harm done this time, so just don't do it again."

"I sure won't. You got my word on that, Mr. Fargo."

"Good enough for me," Fargo said. "Come on. Let's get back to the wagon."

They began working their way toward the road, and

as they walked through the woods, Fargo pointed out the sign that Jonas had left behind him as he followed the deer.

"If you ever find yourself in a situation like that, you can always backtrack and find your way out," he said. Jonas nodded, and Calvin looked pretty interested, too.

Fargo figured they were about a hundred yards away from the road when he heard Junie scream, followed by the pounding of hoofbeats and the sharp, sudden rattle of gunfire.

8

Fargo turned, gripped Jonas' shoulder hard, and said to the boy, "Go behind that big tree and sit down. Don't move, and stay there until one of us comes to get you. Understand?"

Jonas jerked his head in a nod. He looked very frightened again. But he did as Fargo said and sat with his back pressed against the thick trunk of a pine tree. It would protect him from any stray bullets that came whistling into the woods.

Fargo drew his Colt and broke into a run. Calvin was right behind him, Colt Navy in hand. This time Fargo didn't tell him to holster it.

More shooting and yelling came from the road. Fargo heard the popping of handguns, the sharp crack of a rifle, the heavier boom of Bodie's old muzzleloader. He had no doubt about what had happened: Garrett and Joel Braxton, along with their other two friends, had caught up with the wagon and attacked it.

When Fargo and Calvin got close to the road, Fargo dropped into a crouch and motioned for Calvin to do likewise. They crept forward now instead of running, and after a moment Fargo parted some brush and looked out on the scene of battle.

Bodie lay underneath the wagon, firing back up the road. Fargo didn't see any of the children, which gave him reason to hope that Junie had been able to get all of them into the vehicle before the shooting started. The sideboards of the wagon were thick enough to stop at least some of the slugs from the attackers.

The carbine cracked inside the wagon. Fargo didn't know if Junie or Luke was using it, but at least somebody else besides Bodie was putting up a fight. Unfortunately, both the carbine and Bodie's old rifle were single-shot weapons, so they couldn't lay down a very heavy field of fire.

Fargo glanced at the horses and saw the butt of the Henry sticking up from the saddle boot on the Ovaro. If he could get his hands on the repeater, it would certainly help even the odds.

That might not be possible, though, because a hail of bullets sizzled through the space between Fargo and the horses. The shots originated from a clump of rocks about a hundred yards up the road. Fargo saw horses standing with reins dangling at the edge of the trees beyond the rocks.

Puffs of powder smoke came from the hidden gunmen. Fargo knew that the Braxtons and their friends must have charged the wagon, then reined in and taken cover when the resistance from their quarry was heavier than expected.

Now it was a standoff of sorts, but the superior firepower of the enemy meant that in the end the wagon's defenders would be overcome.

Unless Fargo and Calvin did something to change the odds.

"Mr. Fargo, we can't just wait out here and do nothing!" Calvin said as he clutched the sleeve of Fargo's jacket.

"We're not going to," Fargo said as he let the parted brush close up again and backed away from it. "Come on."

Quickly, Fargo and Calvin began to circle to the north, staying off the road and keeping to the trees.

"They probably don't know but what everybody's in the wagon except for Bodie," Fargo said as they hurried through the woods. "We're wild cards in this game, you and me."

When Fargo judged that they had gone far enough, he angled toward the road and motioned for Calvin to follow him. When they reached the edge of the trees, they saw that they were now farther north than the rocks where the gunmen had taken cover.

Those boulders were on the other side of the road, though, so the angle wasn't the best. Fargo caught only glimpses of the men hidden there.

"Aim into those rocks and squeeze off about three shots," he told Calvin.

"But I can't see to aim at them!" the youngster protested.

"Doesn't matter," Fargo assured him. "The bullets will ricochet off the rocks and bounce around a lot. That'll be enough to drive them out. . . ." He lifted his Colt. "And I'll be waiting."

Understanding dawned on Calvin's face. The revolver was fairly steady in his hand as he drew a bead and fired three rounds as fast as he could cock the hammer and pull the trigger.

Fargo heard the high-pitched whine as the bullets ricocheted, followed by yells of alarm from the men hidden in the rocks. One of them stood upright and started to lunge toward the horses.

Before Fargo could fire, Bodie's rifle boomed and the running man's head seemed to explode on his shoulders. Momentum carried him a few more steps before he flopped limply to the ground.

If the other men in the rocks had been about to emerge from cover, that gruesome sight must have made them think twice. But instead they turned their fire away from the wagon and started shooting at the trees where Fargo and Calvin were.

The two of them took cover behind a couple of pines and started pouring lead into the rocks. Calvin had to stop to reload, but Fargo kept up a steady fire until the youngster was ready to join the fight again. Then he thumbed fresh rounds into his Colt while Calvin peppered the rocks with bullets.

Meanwhile, Bodie and whoever was using the carbine continued shooting, so that the men in the rocks were trapped in a rough cross fire. It didn't take long for things to get too hot in there for them to stand.

With the guns in their hands blazing, three men burst out of the rocks and lunged toward the horses. Bullets slammed into the tree trunk close by Fargo's head. He ignored the splinters and chunks of bark flying through the air and coolly drew a bead on one of the men. When he squeezed off a shot, the man spun around and dropped to the ground, hit hard by the Trailsman's bullet.

The other two made it to the horses, though, and leaped wildly into their saddles. Leaning forward, they spurred their mounts into motion and galloped up the road. Fargo and Calvin hurried them along with a few final shots.

"Get your gun reloaded," Fargo told Calvin as the fleeing men rounded a bend in the road and disappeared. "They could double back, and you have to be ready."

Even as he spoke, he was replacing the bullets in his Colt. Snapping the cylinder closed, he stepped out into the road and motioned toward the wagon.

"Get down there and make sure nobody's hurt. Then go get Jonas from where we left him."

Calvin nodded and took off at a run, not wasting

any breath on a reply. Fargo gave a shrill whistle. The Ovaro trotted quickly along the road toward him.

When the stallion reached him, Fargo swung up into the saddle and pulled the Henry from its sheath. Immediately, he felt better about the situation now that he was mounted and had the deadly repeating rifle in his hands.

He backtracked warily up the road, alert for any indication that the gunmen had stopped in their flight and set up an ambush instead. When he swung around the bend, he didn't see them anywhere. He faintly heard the sound of rapid hoofbeats, though. The two who had gotten away were still running.

Fargo turned the stallion and rode quickly back to the wagon. When he got there, he saw all seven of the young'uns gathered around Bodie, who said, "It's just a scratch, dadblast it! I ain't hurt all that bad."

The old-timer had taken off his bearskin coat. The left sleeve of his homespun shirt was stained crimson. "Did they wing you?" Fargo asked without dismounting.

Bodie nodded. "Didn't keep me from shootin' at 'em, though. I got one of the buzzards."

"I know. That was good shooting." Fargo looked over the youngsters and didn't see any sign that anybody was hurt. "None of you kids were hit?"

"We're all fine," Junie said, "thanks to Sally. She was the one who spotted those men first, before they started shooting."

The little girl beamed with pride at the praise.

"Did you get a good enough look at them to recognize any of them?" Fargo asked.

Junie's face was grim as she nodded. "I saw Garrett and Joel. There's no doubt about it. The other two were friends of theirs. I'm not sure about their names, but I know they were there at the farm that night."

"So six out of the eight are done for," Fargo said. "I wonder which two got away."

Calvin suggested, "Let's go have a look while Junie's patchin' up Mr. Strickland's arm."

"You sure you want to do that?" Fargo asked.

The boy nodded. "I can handle it. I've seen worse."

Remembering that they had all witnessed their own father being lynched, Fargo had no doubt what Calvin said was true.

Calvin got on one of the other horses and they rode back to the rocks. The man Bodie had shot lay about twenty feet away; the other dead gunman was ten or fifteen feet beyond him.

Fargo and Calvin dismounted and led the horses over to the fallen men. There wasn't much left of the first man's head. Calvin grimaced and looked sick for a second before he got control of himself.

"That was a fella named Lon Sawyer," the boy said. "Can't really tell that from—from his face, but look at his left hand." Calvin pointed to the outflung left hand, which was missing its little finger. "Sawyer lost that finger in a mill accident. He and Garrett were good friends."

"Was he kin to the Braxtons?"

Calvin shook his head. "Not that I know of."

"How about the other one?"

The second man had fallen facedown on the ground. Fargo hooked the toe of his boot under the man's shoulder and rolled him onto his back. He heard the breath hiss between Calvin's teeth.

"That's Joel," Calvin said in a voice thick with emotion.

Joel Braxton's eyes were wide open, but they would never see anything again. Fargo's bullet had passed through his body, and the bloody froth on Joel's lips told Fargo that he had been shot through the lungs. It had been a hard death, suffocating on his own blood.

But as Fargo remembered everything he had heard about how Joel had enjoyed hanging those innocent men, he couldn't bring himself to feel much sympathy for the young man.

"That means Garrett got away," Fargo mused.

"Yeah," Calvin agreed. "The man with him must've been Johnny Longacre. He was the other one who was there at the farm that night."

"You think Garrett will give up and go home now?"

Calvin looked a little surprised that Fargo was asking his opinion on something important. "I don't know," he said. "Reckon he might, since we've got him outnumbered now. But that would mean goin' back to Black Hugo and admittin' that he'd failed. That might be more dangerous than comin' after us again."

Fargo nodded. He figured it pretty much the same way.

"Go back to the wagon and get the shovel," he said. "We'll get these two buried and then be on our way. I want to reach Springfield today if we can."

A few minutes later, a shovel blade bit into the hard earth with crunching sounds. Fargo and Calvin took turns working steadily and in silence, except when Calvin sighed and said, "I've had to dig too many graves lately."

Fargo just nodded his understanding.

When they were finished, they mounted up and rode back to the wagon. Junie had cleaned and bandaged the wound on Bodie's arm. "It was just a scratch, like Mr. Strickland said," she told Fargo. "I think we were very lucky that no one was hurt worse."

"Let's hope that luck stays with us the rest of the way," Fargo said.

*   *   *

It did, and by that evening, they were rolling into Springfield. There had been no more sign of Garrett Braxton and his surviving companion. Maybe Garrett had given up and gone home.

"You kids know where to find these relatives of yours?" Fargo asked.

"We'll go to Aunt Eula's house first," Junie said. "I've been there, and I remember where it is."

The house was a good-sized one on a side street, with several large trees in the front yard. Fargo thought the three-storied structure looked big enough for all seven of the youngsters. That was a family matter, though, and would have to be worked out among the Haddons.

The woman who answered Fargo's knock on the door was buxom, with quite a bit of gray in her blond hair. She appeared surprised to find a rugged-looking frontiersman in buckskins on her front porch, but she politely asked, "Yes? What can I do for you, sir?"

"Got somebody here with me to see you, ma'am," Fargo told her as he touched the brim of his hat. He moved aside so that the woman could see the children coming up the steps to the porch.

"Land's sake!" she exclaimed as she lifted a hand to her throat. "Junie? Calvin? Is that you? And you've brought all the little ones, too!"

She came out onto the porch to throw her arms around Junie and Calvin and pull them into a hearty embrace. Then she had to exclaim over Luke and Hannah, Jonas and Sally, and finally little Arlo, who was swept up by Aunt Eula and cuddled against her ample bosom.

"My goodness, it's wonderful to see all of you," she said. "Some of you I've never even seen before, but I know all about you." She looked around. "Where's

Walter?" Her gaze landed on Fargo again. "Who are you, sir, and why are you here with these children?"

"Aunt Eula," Junie began, "we've got some bad news. . . ."

"Maybe you folks should all go on inside," Fargo suggested. "There's a lot to talk about, ma'am, but it's a family matter and you don't need me."

He started to step down off the porch.

"Skye!" Junie caught at his arm. "Skye, do you have to go?"

"You're here now," he told her quietly. "You've gotten where you needed to go." All he had to do was to glance at the big, solid house with its warmly glowing windows, and he knew the Haddon youngsters would be all right here. Their aunt would see to that.

"But what are you going to do?"

"I'll get a hotel room and stay around town for a couple of days, just to make sure you're getting settled in. Then I'll be heading north again, I reckon."

Junie caught her lower lip between her teeth for a second. "That's right, you were on your way to Jefferson City when you got saddled with us."

Fargo smiled and said, "I never thought of it like that. Traveling with you folks was a pure pleasure . . . except for when somebody was shooting at us, of course."

"Shooting?" Aunt Eula said. "My Lord, children, what's going on here?"

"Come on, Aunt Eula," Calvin said. "I'll tell you about it."

Junie lingered on the porch while the others went inside. "I should go, too. . . ."

"That's right," Skye said.

"Skye . . . thank you for everything." She came up on her toes and kissed him, resting her hands on his chest as she did so. The kiss was sweet but short, and when she pulled her head back, she said, "I'll never forget you."

"I hope not."

"Will you ever come back this way?"

"You never know," Fargo said. He wasn't in the habit of making promises he might not be able to keep.

Reluctantly, Junie went inside, glancing back at him one final time before she pulled the door closed behind her. Smiling a little sadly, Fargo turned and went back to the road, where he had left Bodie leaning against one of the wagon wheels.

"That gal's really sweet on you," the old-timer said.

"I know. But she'll find some young man here in Springfield and make him mighty happy."

Bodie grunted. "More'n likely." He reached for his mule's reins. "Reckon I'd best be ridin' on. I'll look up my daughter and visit with her for a spell. Where you want to meet up?"

"Meet up for what?" Fargo asked with a frown.

"When you leave here, you're headin' to Braxton's Lick to settle things with Black Hugo and his boy, ain't you?"

Fargo gave a grim chuckle. "Is it that obvious?"

"I told you I've heard stories about you, Fargo. I didn't figure the Trailsman would let Black Hugo get away with tryin' to have a bunch o' young'uns killed."

"I'm going to let the law handle it, if I can."

"That sheriff up yonder ain't gonna do a damned thing, and you know it."

"In that case," Fargo said, "I reckon I'll be justified in defending myself when the Braxtons come after me."

"Well, count me in. It's as much my fight as it is your'n. Maybe more, since I'm the one who's got the sore arm from bein' shot."

"All right," Fargo said as he reached a decision. It wasn't going to do any good to argue with the old pelican. "I'll be at the Maitland Hotel for the next couple of nights. Then I'll head north first thing the next morning."

"I'll be there."

Bodie stuck out a gnarled hand, and Fargo shook with him. He was glad Bodie was going along. The old-timer was a good man in a fight, and there was no telling how many killers Black Hugo Braxton could round up on the other side.

Before this was over, Fargo was liable to need all the help he could get.

He was surprised, late that night, just before he was about to turn in, when a soft knock sounded on the door of his room in the Maitland Hotel. He had already taken off his shirt, along with his gun belt, but still wore the buckskin trousers.

Snagging the Colt from the holster where the gun belt hung over the back of a chair, Fargo went to the door and called through the panel, "Who is it?"

As soon as the words were out of his mouth, he stepped quickly to one side, in case whoever was out there in the hall tried to shoot through the door.

"Junie Haddon," came the soft reply.

Fargo frowned and opened the door. Junie stood there in the hallway, alone. She had a flushed but happy look on her face.

"Come in," Fargo said as he lowered the gun. "What are you doing here?"

Junie came into the room. She wore a simple gray dress and had a lace shawl over her fair hair. "I wanted to let you know," she said, "that Aunt Eula has asked all of us to live with her. She has plenty of room because she's a widow, and her own kids are grown up and moved out. We're not going to be split up, Skye."

Fargo smiled. "That's good news. I appreciate you telling me. I'm a mite curious, though, how you knew where to find me."

"I overheard what you told Mr. Strickland about staying here. I—I'm afraid I slipped back onto the porch and eavesdropped. I thought maybe you would tell him what your plans were."

Fargo tensed. Did she know that he was going after Black Hugo and Garrett Braxton? She didn't act like it, but he couldn't tell for sure.

"I went back inside after I heard you say that you were going to be staying here at the Maitland Hotel," she went on, indirectly answering the question that had gone through Fargo's mind. "I wasn't really planning to come see you so soon, but . . . but I kept thinking about it . . . about you. . . ."

Fargo was aware that he was naked from the waist up, and that Junie's eyes kept playing across his broad, muscular chest. He put the Colt back in its holster and reached for his shirt. "I'll take you back to your aunt Eula's place," he said as he started to shrug into the garment.

"No!" She stepped closer to him and rested a hand on his bare chest. "No, not yet, Skye. There are other things I want to say . . . and do."

He looked into her eyes and said, "We've had this conversation before, back at Bear Creek, remember? You don't owe me a thing, and certainly not that."

"It's not a matter of owing you." She moved still closer to him, so that he felt the warmth of her breath on his skin. "It's a matter of wanting you. Ever since I first saw you, Skye, I've had this feeling inside . . . this longing that it's going to take you to satisfy."

"The first time you saw me," Fargo pointed out,

"you were just about frozen and half-starved to death. I don't reckon you were thinking about such things right then."

"Well, then, by that night I knew it," she said with a slight frown of impatience. "You remember that night, don't you?"

The memory of how she had looked standing nude in front of the fireplace in the roadhouse was etched into Fargo's brain and probably always would be. "I remember," he said quietly.

Both of her hands were on his chest now as she leaned closer to him. "I may not like to cuss, but I'm still a hill girl. I know what goes on between a man and a woman. And I want that, Skye. I want it with you. But I make no promises beyond tonight."

"I wouldn't expect you to."

"Nor would I expect you to. Simple, isn't it?"

Only it was never that simple, and Fargo knew it.

But he also knew that he couldn't turn Junie away a second time. He wanted her as much as she wanted him. Because she was always with her brothers and sisters, he sometimes thought of her as a youngster, too, but she was really a full-grown woman.

Right now she was a full-grown woman in desperate need of some loving, and she proved it by lifting her mouth to Fargo's and planting a hot, urgent kiss on him. Her tongue darted boldly between his lips. Her hands moved on his bare chest.

Fargo's arms went around her and pulled her closer. He was gentle about it, as gentle as he could be considering the passion that surged up inside him. He didn't know how much experience Junie had, if any, and he didn't want to do anything that would mar her memories of this night.

Slowly, sensuously, he undressed her. The wick of the lamp on the bedside table was turned low, and she was as lovely in its warm yellow glow as she had been by the light of the flames in the roadhouse fireplace.

If anything she was even more beautiful now because she no longer showed the strain of walking halfway across the Ozarks in the dead of winter. She had a healthy vitality about her that made Fargo want to laugh with joy.

When he was naked, too, she looked down at his erect member and ran her fingers along the thick, iron-hard shaft. "It's beautiful," she breathed.

"*You're* beautiful," Fargo told her. He lowered her to the bed.

For long minutes, they lay there caressing and exploring each other. Judging by Junie's eagerness and awe, this might indeed be the first time she had experienced these sensations. Fargo had bedded a few virgins in his life, but for the most part the women he'd been with had been more . . . well, seasoned, he thought.

The wondrousness of it was all new to Junie, though, and Fargo felt revitalized by her innocent, boundless lust. When he moved between her widespread thighs and she gripped him eagerly and brought him to her opening, she gasped, "Now, Skye, please take me now!"

He obliged with a slow, steady thrust of his hips that sheathed him fully inside her. She cried out softly and pumped her hips in the instinctive motion of a woman accepting a man into her body. Fargo pulled back and then surged forward again, taking it nice and easy.

In and out he drove, withdrawing until the connection between them was almost broken, then plunging deeply within her again. She wrapped her arms and legs around him and clung tightly as his hips bobbed up and down. Passion made her nip at his shoulder before their lips met again in a kiss. Their tongues dueled, invading each other's mouth in turn.

Fargo made it last, fighting down the urge to climax that swept through him on more than one occasion. He wanted this to be memorable for Junie. Spasms rippled through her and she cried out in culmination, but Fargo kept up the steady rhythm, pausing only briefly to let her catch her breath before lifting her higher and still higher.

Finally, holding back was no longer possible, and as Junie began to shudder again in yet another climax, Fargo buried his manhood as deeply inside her as it would go and let loose, pumping his juices into her in spurt after searing spurt.

Junie clasped him tightly as the last of her spasms shook her. Fargo stayed where he was for a long moment but finally withdrew from her and rolled onto his back, taking her with him so that she sprawled on top of him. He pulled the covers over them so they wouldn't get chilled.

"It was better than I ever dreamed it could be, Skye," she whispered. "I just wish I could spend the night so we could do that over and over again."

"I do, too," Fargo said. "You'll have to get back to your aunt's before somebody realizes you're gone, though."

"You'll take me there?"

"Of course."

"Then don't say anything more about it for a few minutes. I want to lie here for a little while longer." Her lips brushed his. "I'll never forget this night, Skye. Never."

Fargo had a feeling that he wouldn't, either.

After escorting Junie back to her aunt's house—where she climbed a tree and went back in the same window she had left from, all with an endearing, tomboyish grace—Fargo returned to the hotel and slept soundly.

He didn't get up until late the next morning, and after eating breakfast he walked down the street to the livery stable where he had left the Ovaro and checked on the big stallion. Then he visited the local telegraph office and sent a wire to Ed Morrisey in Jefferson City, advising his friend that he had been delayed but would get there sooner or later. Fargo also told Morrisey to go ahead with the plans without him if he needed to.

What with one thing and another, such as selling the wagon and the mules and getting back some of the money he had spent, it was late in the day before Fargo headed back over to Aunt Eula's house. Even if Garrett Braxton and Johnny Longacre had followed the youngsters to Springfield, Fargo didn't think they would try anything in the middle of a busy, respectable neighborhood such as the one where Eula lived.

He wanted to be sure of that, though, so that he could rest easier. And if he was honest with himself, which he tried to be, he knew that he wanted to see Junie again, too.

But Fargo wasn't prepared for the sight of Luke Haddon's face when the boy opened the door to his knock. Fargo knew instantly that something was wrong.

"Mr. Fargo!" Luke exclaimed. His face was as drawn and worried as Fargo had ever seen it, even when he had first met the youngsters. "Thank God, you're here! We didn't know where you were staying, but I was about to come lookin' for you anyway."

Fargo stepped into the foyer and asked, "What's wrong?"

"It's Calvin and Junie. . . . They're gone!" Luke

raked his fingers through his sandy hair. "They're both gone!"

Fargo gripped the boy's arm to steady him. He needed Luke to be calm and tell him what had happened. "Was it Garrett Braxton?"

"No." Luke shook his head. "They took the horses. Calvin left first, and when Junie found out, she went after him. None of us knew about it at first, but then Hannah found the note Junie left. . . ."

Fargo reined in his impatience at Luke's rambling. "Where did they go?"

"Back home," Luke said hollowly. "Back to Braxton's Lick. Calvin went to kill Black Hugo, and Junie went after him to try to stop him and bring him back!"

9

Self-recrimination wasn't going to do any good, Fargo knew. He could kick himself all day and half the night, and it wouldn't help him keep Junie and Calvin from getting themselves killed.

In the parlor with Aunt Eula and the other Haddon children, Fargo looked at the note Junie had left. It explained that she had discovered Calvin missing from his room early that morning. The horse he had ridden was gone, too, and so was the Colt Navy Fargo had bought for him.

Junie had drawn the only conclusion she could: Calvin had set off on a mission of revenge directed at the Braxtons.

It was a damned foolish thing to do, of course. Calvin thought he was getting pretty good with that gun, and with a young man's confidence, he had decided to settle the score and avenge his father's death. Junie, always the big sister, had gone after him.

Fargo handed the note back to Eula to keep from crumpling the paper in his frustration. Why hadn't Junie come back to the hotel and told him what was going on? He could have caught up to Calvin and talked some sense into the boy's head. Failing that, he would have brought him back to Springfield anyway.

But now they had almost an entire day's lead on him, and although the Ovaro was fast and strong, it wouldn't be easy to erase that margin.

Fargo looked at Luke. "Tomorrow morning, Bodie Strickland is supposed to meet me at the Maitland Hotel. Find him and tell him what's happened. He can head for Braxton's Lick if he wants to; it's up to him."

"Where will you be?" Luke asked.

"Already on my way there. I'm leaving as soon as I can put some supplies together."

"I've got plenty of food on hand here," Eula said. "Why don't you just take what you need, Mr. Fargo?"

Fargo thought it over for a second and then nodded his thanks. That would speed things up considerably.

Dusk was settling over the city by the time he was ready to leave. He wouldn't be able to travel all night, but he wanted to put some miles behind him, anyway, before he made camp. Maybe he could shave a few miles off the lead the youngsters had on him.

When he opened the front door to go out onto the porch, he stopped short at the sight of Bodie coming up the steps. The old-timer stopped, too, and looked surprised at the grim expression on Fargo's face.

"What's wrong?" Bodie asked.

"Calvin ran off to Braxton's Lick to have it out with Black Hugo and Garrett," Fargo said. "Junie went after him. What are you doing here, Bodie?"

"Just thought I'd come by and see how them young-'uns was doin'." Bodie scratched at his beard and grimaced. "To tell you the truth, I ain't sure my gal was all that happy to see me on her doorstep last night. She ain't used to havin' an old badger like me around. It didn't take us long to catch up." He squared his shoulders. "So I reckon I'm goin' with you after them kids."

Fargo clapped a hand on the old man's bony shoulder. "Sounds good to me. I'll be glad to have you along. Are you ready to ride now?"

"Durned tootin'."

Fargo turned to Luke, who had followed him into the foyer. "You won't have to meet Bodie in the morning. He's here now."

"All right," Luke said. "Mr. Fargo . . . how about takin' me with you?"

Fargo frowned. "You're only fourteen."

"I can handle a gun, though," Luke said quickly. "Maybe not as good as Calvin yet, but he let me shoot that Navy of his a few times. I can help you if you have to fight the Braxtons."

"You can help more by staying here and taking care of your brothers and sisters," Fargo told him firmly.

"But—"

Fargo shook his head. "That's final, Luke, and don't start thinking that you can follow Bodie and me and we won't send you back. We will, but you'll just slow us down."

"All right," Luke said reluctantly. "Just one thing, Mr. Fargo."

"What's that?"

"Don't let anything happen to Junie and Calvin."

"I'll do my best," Fargo promised.

And if anything bad did happen to those youngsters, he would see that the men responsible paid for it—with their lives.

A cold wind sprang up as Fargo and Bodie left Springfield heading north. The road was easy enough to follow, even in the dark. The moon was only a thin crescent, but there were millions of stars to light their way.

But then those stars and the sliver of moon were swallowed up by thick clouds moving in, and the air grew colder. The few days of warmer weather were over. They had been only a brief respite from the bitter winter.

"That boy's a damned fool," Bodie muttered. "Had himself a good place to stay, an' he has to go and do somethin' foolish like this."

"He's got a boy's pride," Fargo said. "I know it's been eating at him that he had to stand by and do nothing while his father was taken out and lynched. That would bother me, too."

"Yeah, I reckon. Still, he oughta knowed he can't go up against the Braxtons by himself."

Fargo couldn't argue with that. He knew, though, that sometimes hate had a life of its own, more powerful than anything mortal man could bring against it. In the case of the Braxtons and the Haddons, that hatred had been festering for so long it was like a living, breathing thing, and Calvin had succumbed to its siren song.

This was a blood feud, and the only thing that could answer the call of blood was more blood.

The cold and the stygian darkness finally forced Fargo and Bodie to pull off the road, find some trees and brush that would serve as a windbreak, and roll up in their blankets to spend a few frigid, miserable hours trying to sleep. Both men were still weary when the gray light of dawn spread over the Missouri landscape and they rode north again.

The trail hugged the base of the Ozarks to the west and sometimes twisted through rugged, heavily wooded foothills. Fargo and Bodie pushed their mounts as hard as they could, but there was only so much ground even the Trailsman's gallant Ovaro and

Bodie's sturdy mule could cover in a day. Still, Fargo was confident that they were cutting into the lead Junie and Calvin had on them.

They hadn't caught up by the time an early dusk descended, however, and their mounts had to have rest. Although he was frustrated, Fargo knew that riding the Ovaro and the mule into the ground wouldn't help any.

They had passed the Forrest farm earlier in the day and stopped long enough to ask Howard Forrest if he had seen the two youngsters. Forrest had just shaken his head, though. "If they came by this way, they didn't stop, Mr. Fargo," he'd said.

Fargo wasn't surprised. Forrest knew what had happened up at Braxton's Lick. If he had seen either Calvin or Junie headed in that direction, he might have tried to stop them.

Fargo wondered if they were still traveling separately, or if Junie had caught up to Calvin. He hoped the latter was true. That would mean they might be headed south again, if Junie had been able to talk some sense into Calvin's head.

Also, Fargo didn't like the idea of Junie riding through the Ozarks alone. A lot of things could happen to a young, pretty girl on her own in a rough land, and mighty few of them were good.

His worry grew as another cold, gray day went by and he and Bodie reached Bear Creek. As they reined to a halt in front of the blackened ruins that had been Grundy's roadhouse, Fargo shook his head at the destruction. Too many people had died, too many lives had been damaged.

All because of an old grudge, the cause of which nobody even remembered!

"Hey! Hey, Mr. Fargo!"

Turning quickly in the saddle, Fargo saw that Hank

Merriman had come out onto the porch of his store across the road. The fire had been confined to the roadhouse; it hadn't spread to the store and the church.

Fargo turned the Ovaro and walked the stallion across the road, followed by Bodie. Merriman had a piece of paper in his hand. He held it up toward Fargo as he said, "Those fellas told me you'd be along sooner or later. They said for me to give you this." Merriman had a few beads of sweat on his forehead despite the chilly, overcast day. "Said if I didn't, they'd come back and give me some o' what Grundy and Lizbeth got."

A thin skim of ice had formed around the edges of the water in the trough in front of the store, but the feeling that went down Fargo's spine at that moment was even colder. "Where are Grundy and Lizbeth?" he asked as he took the folded paper from Merriman.

"Gone," the storekeeper said. "Once they got over the worst of the beatin' those bastards gave 'em, Lizbeth said they were gonna go somewhere else and start over. I don't know where they went, though. I just wished 'em well."

So did Fargo, but right now he was more concerned with the contents of the note that Merriman had just given him. He reached down and drew his Arkansas toothpick from its sheath. With the tip of the blade, he pried loose the wax that sealed the paper shut, then replaced the big knife.

He unfolded the paper and saw words scrawled on it.

THOSE TWO KIDS WILL DIE IF YOU DON'T COME TO BRAXTON'S LICK. YOU CAN FIND THEM AT THE HADDON PLACE.

"What's it say?" Bodie asked. "I never did get round to learnin' how to read."

Fargo read the message aloud, and the old-timer cursed sulfurously. "Who done this?" he demanded. "Who's got them young'uns?"

Merriman rubbed his chin and said nervously, "I'm pretty sure it was Black Hugo Braxton. I never saw him before, but I've heard him described plenty of times. He had five or six men with him, and I think one of them was his son."

Fargo nodded. Garrett hadn't had time to return to Braxton's Lick, fetch his father and some reinforcements, and return to points south of Bear Creek.

The only explanation that made sense was if Hugo had decided to follow his sons and make sure they carried out his orders. He could have run into Garrett while the younger man was riding back to Braxton's Lick and forced him to turn around and start toward Springfield again.

Then, in a cruel twist of fate, they had run right into Calvin and Junie and taken them prisoner. Now they were using the two youngsters to lure Fargo and Bodie into danger.

"Does Hugo Braxton know who I am?" Fargo asked Merriman.

"He must've forced those kids to tell him who helped them get away before. He told me to be sure to give that note to Skye Fargo."

Fargo nodded, folded the note, and slipped it into the pocket of his coat. Black Hugo must be figuring that Fargo, Bodie, and the two older Haddon siblings represented the real threat to him. The law wouldn't listen to anything Luke and the younger ones had to say. If Hugo could get rid of Calvin and Junie, along with Fargo and Bodie, then he could rest easy about the authorities coming after him for the lynching of Walter Haddon and the other three men.

Hugo's name was on that official complaint, Fargo

recalled. In the eyes of the law, he would bear plenty of the blame for what had happened, even though Garrett and Joel had come up with the plan.

Hugo had to know by now, too, that Joel was dead, and that Fargo had killed him.

That was just one more blood debt for Black Hugo Braxton to settle with more killing, Fargo told himself.

"Much obliged," Fargo said as he turned the Ovaro into the face of the wind again. Bodie did likewise with his mule.

"Where are you going?" Merriman called after them.

"Braxton's Lick," Fargo replied, but for all he knew, the words were carried away by the howling of the norther.

In a way, knowing that Junie and Calvin were Black Hugo's prisoners was a relief. Braxton would keep them alive as long as there was a chance he might need to use them against Fargo and Bodie. Fargo could stop worrying about some other mishap befalling the two youngsters.

But he had plenty of other things to worry about, such as the treatment they were receiving at the hands of their captors, and that gnawed at him during the next day and a half as he and Bodie pushed their mounts hard toward Braxton's Lick.

As they approached the settlement around dusk, Fargo sensed eyes watching them from the woods, as well as from the farmhouses they passed. A tense anticipation seemed to have settled over the land, along with cold air and thick gray clouds. More than once, Fargo and Bodie saw farmers hurrying into their houses and shutting the doors solidly, as if they wanted no part of the two men riding by outside.

So this was what it felt like to be a pariah, Fargo

told himself grimly. The people around here knew what Black Hugo was up to. They knew that Fargo and Bodie were riding to their deaths. At least, that was what Hugo Braxton intended.

Fargo and Bodie planned to have something to say about that.

They came up behind a farmer driving a cart along the road. The man looked over his shoulder, saw them coming, and tried to lash his mule into a faster gait. Fargo heeled the Ovaro into a trot and rode up alongside the cart before the farmer could get away. He leaned over and grasped the mule's harness, pulling the animal to a halt.

"Please, mister," the farmer pleaded. "Just ride on. Don't stop here."

"Tell me where to find the Haddon place, and I'll be on my way."

The farmer swallowed hard and nodded. "S-sure. Go on up this road"—he pointed with a trembling finger—"about another mile. You'll come to a little crossroad. Take the turn to the left. The Haddon farm's about five hundred yards along that lane. You can't miss it."

Fargo let go of the harness. "Much obliged." He turned to his companion, who had caught up while Fargo was talking to the farmer. "Come on, Bodie."

They left the frightened farmer behind them, pale and trembling, as if the black wings of the death angel had been hovering over him, too.

Fargo and Bodie found the crossroad without any trouble and turned left into the lane. Quietly, Fargo said, "The deck must be stacked pretty high against us, the way folks around here are acting."

"Yeah, but I've played long odds before and won. I reckon you have, too, Fargo."

"That's right," Fargo said with a nod.

"I ain't foolish enough to believe that we'll win just because we got right on our side, though. It'll take plenty o' fast shootin' and a steady eye, too. Maybe a mite o' luck."

"I'll take all we can get."

Fargo reined in sharply as several figures on horseback loomed up in the lane in front of them. "Hold it right there!" a voice called.

Somebody lit a torch. By its flaring light, Fargo saw a badge pinned to the coat of the man who had challenged them. He said, "You'd be Sheriff Reynolds?"

The man jerked his head in a nod. "That's right. Ain't nothin' up this road you men need to see tonight. Better turn around and ride away."

Fargo held the stallion's reins in his left hand and kept his right close to the butt of his Colt. "You know we can't do that, Sheriff. I'm a little surprised Braxton sent you out here to stop us. I thought he wanted his showdown."

"Hugo didn't send me," Reynolds said. "I came on my own. There's been enough killin'. It's time for it to stop."

"Enough killing," Fargo repeated. "You mean like the night Walter Haddon and his friends were strung up, even though they were innocent?"

Fargo saw the conflict on the sheriff's weathered face. Oliver Reynolds had sworn to uphold the law, but his loyalty to the Braxtons had forced him to shatter that oath. From the looks of his miserable expression, that betrayal was eating at his guts.

"There's nothin' I can do to change the past," Reynolds said after a long moment of strained silence. "But if you'll turn around, mister, I'll see if I can't go and get Hugo to turn those kids loose. You got my word on it."

Fargo considered the offer, but only for a second.

Then he shook his head and said, "You might try to reason with Braxton, Sheriff, but in the end you'll go along with what he wants. We both know it."

Anger flared on Reynolds' face. "Damn it—" Then he stopped and drew a deep breath. "You're right," he said hollowly. He looked down at the front of his coat. "This badge don't mean a thing anymore."

With that, he ripped the badge off and threw it on the ground.

"Let 'em pass, boys," he said to his deputies. "That's my last order as sheriff."

Slowly, the deputies moved their horses aside so that Fargo and Bodie could ride on.

As they passed Reynolds, Fargo thought he heard the man murmur, "Good luck."

They were close now. Fargo could sense it. He and Bodie pushed their mounts into a trot. As they rode around a bend in the trail, they saw the Haddon farmhouse up ahead. The windows were ablaze with light. Every lamp in the place must be lit.

And on the front porch, on either side of the door, two people sat in cane-bottomed chairs. Fargo recognized Junie and Calvin. From their awkward, uncomfortable-looking positions, he knew they were tied into the chairs.

No one else was in sight, but as Fargo and Bodie approached and slowed the Ovaro and the mule to a walk, the front door opened with a squeal of hinges and a man stepped outside. He was medium-sized, not all that impressive physically, but the jutting white beard and the flowing white hair told Fargo he was looking at Black Hugo Braxton.

The man's actions had played a major part in Fargo's life for the past two weeks, yet this was the first time Fargo had laid eyes on him. Braxton wore a dark, sober suit and a broad-brimmed black hat. He looked more like a preacher than the evil patriarch of a murderous family.

But as Fargo and Bodie came closer, Fargo saw the insane hatred blazing in Black Hugo's eyes. The man had a short-barreled shotgun in his right hand, the butt propped against his hip. He lifted his left hand, as if performing a benediction, as the two riders reined to a stop in front of the porch.

Calvin and Junie were both gagged as well as tied. They made frantic noises behind the gags. Fargo thought they were trying to tell him and Bodie to whirl their mounts and gallop away while they still had the chance. That wasn't going to happen, of course.

"Fargo," Black Hugo intoned in a deep, sonorous voice, making him seem more than ever like a preacher, "I knew you'd come. The lives of these children hung in the balance."

"We're here now," Fargo said. "Why don't you let them go, and you and I can settle what's between us?"

"The death of my youngest son, you mean? The foul murder of my boy?"

"Jocl was doing his damnedest to kill those youngsters. I'm not going to apologize for shooting him, if that's what you're waiting for."

Braxton's left hand was still upraised. He lowered it now, and as if following a stage cue, small, gritty snowflakes began to drift down.

Men carrying rifles and shotguns stepped out from the corners of the house and emerged from the trees next to what was left of the burned-down barn. Fargo looked around and quickly counted eight men, including Black Hugo. Garrett Braxton came out of the house to stand behind his father, making the odds nine against two.

Long odds, as Bodie had said. They had no choice but to play the hand as it was dealt, though.

"If you and your friend want to make your peace with the Lord, Fargo, now's the time," Black Hugo said.

Bodie leaned over in the saddle and spat. "That's rich," he said. "The Devil hisownself tellin' me to make my peace with the Lord."

Braxton's bearded jaw tightened.

"What are you going to tell the sheriff?" Fargo asked, his voice ringing out loud and clear in the chilly night. "Reynolds let your boys get away with lynching Walter Haddon and his friends, but how are you going to claim this is anything but murder?"

Black Hugo laughed harshly. "Oliver Reynolds is part of the family. Besides that, he's a gutless coward. He'll do anything I tell him to do and accept any story I give him." Scorn dripped from Braxton's voice. "I'm not worried about the sheriff."

Fargo had heard the solitary set of hoofbeats following him and Bodie as they approached the farm a few minutes earlier. He had played a hunch, had counted on his impressions of the tortured state of Oliver Reynolds' heart and soul. He had prodded the contemptuous words out of Black Hugo in hopes that they would finally force Reynolds to face up to what he had become. . . .

And as the sheriff suddenly spurred out of the darkness with a hoarse shout and as Colt flame bloomed from the gun clutched in his hand, Fargo knew his gamble had paid off.

Reynolds swept down on Braxton's gunmen, trampling one of them and blasting two more off their feet. At the same instant, Fargo jabbed his heels into the Ovaro's flanks and sent the stallion leaping up the steps onto the porch itself. With startled yells, Black Hugo and Garrett flung themselves out of the way of the big horse, retreating into the house.

Fargo's left foot came out of the stirrup and kicked the chair where Junie was tied, toppling it to the floor of the porch. He had to hope that would keep her out of the way of most of the bullets that would be flying around.

Garrett appeared in the window behind Calvin, smashing out the glass with his six-gun and drawing a bead on the boy's head. Bodie fired first, the old muzzle-loader in his hands belching flame. Garrett doubled over as the slug struck him high in the belly. The gun in his hand exploded, but the barrel was pointed at the porch now and the bullet buried itself harmlessly in the thick planks. Garrett dropped the gun and sagged forward through the broken window, not noticing how the jagged glass cut into his flesh. He couldn't feel it.

Fargo wheeled the stallion, the big horse turning sharply even in the close confines of the porch. The Colt in his hand bucked as he triggered several shots at the men charging toward the house. A couple of them staggered and went down, but two more came on. Fargo leaped the Ovaro off the porch. The stallion crashed through the flimsy railing, and the two Braxton men screamed as iron-shod hooves slashed at them. The Ovaro trampled right over them.

That left only Black Hugo Braxton, and Fargo had to roll out of the saddle as Black Hugo charged from the house and fired one barrel of the shotgun at him. The buckshot screamed through the air above the Ovaro's back, narrowly missing the stallion.

Fargo landed hard on the ground. The impact jarred the revolver out of his hand. Black Hugo stalked down off the porch and came toward Fargo. "Stay back!" he yelled at Bodie and Reynolds. "Stay back or I'll blow his damned head off!"

Fargo glanced at the Colt he had dropped. One fast

move would bring him within reach of it. But no matter how fast he was, he wouldn't be able to grab the Colt before Black Hugo could jerk the shotgun's trigger. Nor could he reach the Arkansas toothpick in time.

Movement from the porch caught his eye. He saw that when Junie's chair had fallen over, the back of it had cracked and broken. She had been able to pull her arms free. Dragging the chair behind her since her legs were still tied to it, she lunged across the porch toward the gun Garrett had dropped.

Black Hugo heard the clatter and turned, bringing the shotgun around. Fargo threw himself forward and snatched up his Colt. On the porch, Junie got her hands on Garrett's gun and tipped up the barrel, pulling back the hammer as she did so. Bodie jerked his reloaded rifle to his shoulder, and Reynolds leveled his handgun.

All the weapons went off so close together it sounded like one huge explosion. Clouds of powder smoke rolled across the yard in front of the house. Black Hugo Braxton came up on his toes and arched his back as lead tore into him from four different directions at once. It was almost like the impacts cancelled themselves out and held up Braxton's bullet-riddled body for a long second. The shotgun slipped from his fingers and thudded to the ground.

Braxton followed it a heartbeat later, landing in a limp sprawl. A black pool began to form underneath him and spread slowly around him.

Fargo leaped up and bounded onto the porch. He reached down and ripped the gag from Junie's mouth. "Are you all right?" he asked urgently. "Were you hit?"

"I—I'm fine, Skye," she gasped. "What about . . . Calvin?"

Fargo looked at the boy, who stared back at him

wide-eyed. Fargo didn't see any blood on Calvin's clothes. Calvin nodded to indicate that he wasn't hurt.

"Looks like that shotgun blast just hit the edge of the porch," Bodie commented as he pointed to a ragged hole chewed into the planks. "Whoa! What the hell!"

Sheriff Reynolds had fallen off his horse, landing almost at Bodie's feet.

Bodie knelt next to the lawman while Fargo cut Junie and Calvin loose with his knife. The old-timer pulled back Reynolds' coat and exposed a bloodstain on the man's shirt. "Reckon I got . . . hit," Reynolds grunted.

Fargo came down the steps to join Bodie. "It don't look too bad," Bodie said. "Took some hide and a little chunk o' meat outta the sheriff's side, but he oughta be all right if we get him into the settlement and let a sawbones tend to him."

Reynolds raised a hand. "Fargo," he said. "Fargo, I'm—I'm sorry I let things . . . get this far. . . ."

"You should have put a stop to what Black Hugo was doing a long time ago," Fargo said bluntly. Then his tone softened a little as he added, "But at least you finally took a stand. Maybe you ought to find that badge you threw down and pin it on again."

Reynolds shook his head. "Too late . . . for that. But maybe one of these days . . . at least I'll be able to live with myself . . . again. . . ."

Fargo and Bodie helped the wounded sheriff to his feet while Junie and Calvin rounded up all the horses, including the ones the Braxton men had left tied up and hidden in the trees. They got Reynolds onto his mount and then went onto the porch to pull Garrett Braxton's body through the broken window and lay him next to his father. With that done, everyone who was still alive swung up into their own saddles.

Except for Junie, who hurried back into the house.

Fargo didn't know what she was doing. A moment later she reappeared, carrying a lamp. She paused just outside the open front door.

"Junie," Calvin said. "What—"

"This isn't our home anymore, Calvin," she said. "And the good memories of this place can't compete with all the tragedy it's seen. Whoever winds up with the land, it won't be the Haddons. The new owners should start fresh, and so should we."

Calvin looked at his sister as several seconds went by, and then he nodded. "Do it," he said.

Junie pulled back her arm and threw the lamp into the house. Fargo heard the tinkle of glass as it broke. With a whoosh, the spilled oil caught fire, and flames began to spread rapidly as Junie turned and came down the steps. The doorway behind her filled with a garish glow.

Fargo held out a hand. Junie took it, and he lifted her to the Ovaro's back, cradling her in front of the saddle. "Let's go," he said. As the riders turned away, the snow began to fall harder, swirling down thickly from the black winter sky.

But no matter how hard it fell, the snow was no match for the cleansing flames.

LOOKING FORWARD!

**The following is the opening
section of the next novel in the exciting
Trailsman series from Signet:**

THE TRAILSMAN #294
OREGON OUTLAWS

*Oregon Territory, 1860—
grizzly bears, escaped prisoners, and a crooked
town. The Trailsman will fight them all, but
can he win?*

The grizzly came barreling out of the trees at a dead
run, a big silvertip, seven hundred pounds of muscle,
hide, hair, claws, and teeth.

Later, when he had the time to think about it, the
man with the lake blue eyes wondered where the bear
had come from and what had stirred it up so. There
was no cub nearby, not that Skye Fargo had noticed,
and he was a man who noticed just about everything.

He'd seen no claw marks on the trees, nor anything else to signal that a bear was in the vicinity.

Fargo had walked down to the little stream for a quick wash before making camp. He'd laid his rifle aside, and there was no way of getting to it. Maybe the bear was upset because it had been about to catch a fish for its supper and Fargo had gotten in the way.

Not that it really mattered what had riled the bear. What mattered was that it was madder than hell and had its eyes set on Fargo.

There was nowhere to run, and no time for running even if an escape route had been available. Fargo didn't even have time to pull his pistol. He could have dropped down and pretended to be dead, hoping the bear wouldn't kill him immediately, but the grizzly was too angry to care if he was dead or alive. It was going to punish him no matter what condition he was in.

So when the bear was within a couple of feet of him, Fargo jumped to the side. The bear had worked up such a head of steam that it almost went right past him and into the water, but it managed to lash out with one huge paw and swat Fargo on the back.

Fargo heard his buckskins tearing and felt the searing burn of the claws as they raked his shoulder and upper arm. Then he was flying through the air.

He landed about ten yards away from where the bear was making a turn at the edge of the stream. Grabbing for his pistol, Fargo discovered that it was gone. The grizzly's blow had jolted it from the holster, and Fargo couldn't see where it had landed.

The only defense Fargo had left was his Arkansas toothpick, the sharp knife that had saved him from more foes than one. But not from anything as ferocious and enormous as the bear that was coming at him now.

The grizzly's head swung from side to side and its eyes seemed to glow with its hatred of Fargo, but at least it wasn't coming as fast as it had the first time. Fargo had a little time to think of what he might do.

Thinking, however, didn't help. The bear was simply too big, too strong, too fast. Fargo had no time for planning. He had to act.

When the grizzly came so close that Fargo could smell its meaty breath, he jabbed it in the muzzle with the knife.

The bear jerked in surprise. It didn't appear any more hurt than Fargo would have been hurt by a wasp sting. And it didn't get calmer. If anything, it was more agitated than before.

Fargo felt the warm blood running from the places where the claws had sliced him, and pain lanced through him. He kept the knife ready.

The bear came at him again. Fargo jabbed it in the muzzle and jumped aside.

The grizzly roared and turned toward him, baring its sharp teeth, saliva flying, but Fargo didn't retreat. Instead he jumped forward, ducked to the side, grabbed a handful of the bear's fur, and pulled himself up onto its back.

For a moment, the bear didn't move. Then it hurled itself erect on its hind legs, throwing its front paws and head straight toward the clouds as it roared at the sky.

Fargo tightened his hold on the bear's rough fur. The animal's rank smell engulfed Fargo as he laid his head against it, trying to grip with his legs as well as his hand. He didn't have much luck, so he put the knife between his teeth and held tight with both hands.

The bear tried to shake him off as if he were some troublesome insect, and Fargo clung like a tick. He wondered if anyone had ever ridden a bear before. Anyone who had lived to tell about it, that is.

Not having any luck bouncing Fargo from its back, the grizzly headed for the trees at a jarring lope. With every step, Fargo felt the blood pump out of him.

Fargo thought about letting go and sliding to the ground, but he knew that if he did, the bear would round on him and attack again. He would wait to see what the bear had in mind.

It had decided to rake him off by rubbing against a tree.

Fargo had a couple of choices. He could try to get off the bear and up into the tree. If he did that, he'd have to take the chance that the bear didn't decide to come after him, but his other choice was to hang on, hope the bear didn't crush him, then try to kill it.

Killing the grizzly with a knife might have been possible, but Fargo didn't have the strength left to try it. He was weakened by loss of blood and by the painful blow the bear had given him. He decided to climb the tree if he could reach a limb.

He could. Before the bear even had a chance to start rubbing, Fargo managed to grasp a sturdy branch and pull himself into the tree. He was able to clamber off the bear's back and up the trunk for eight or ten feet before the bear was quite aware of what was happening.

Blood dripped down from Fargo's wound and got the bear's attention, eliciting a furious growl as the bear started up the tree.

But the limbs were too small to hold the grizzly's weight, and the trunk was too thin to allow its claws much of a purchase. The bear slid to the ground and shook the tree. By that time, Fargo was sitting on a limb with his legs wrapped around the trunk. He wasn't going anywhere.

The grizzly didn't give up easily. It roared and grumbled, walked away and came back, bumped the tree and lashed it with its claws, sending the bark flying.

Fargo closed his eyes, leaned on the trunk, and held on tight.

After what seemed like a very long time, the grizzly gave one final roar, looked up at Fargo with burning eyes, and shambled back into the trees.

Fargo stayed where he was for another half hour, until he was convinced the bear was gone for good. Then he climbed down the tree.

He was surprised by how weak he was, especially his arm, and he wondered how much blood he had lost. His buckskin shirt was soaked with it.

When he reached the ground, his knees were wobbly. He walked unsteadily to the stream and looked around for his pistol. When he found it, he replaced it in the holster.

Fargo peeled off his shirt and inspected it. It was badly torn, and so was the skin on his back and shoulder. The nearest doctor was back in Portland, which Fargo had left the day before after leading a group of pilgrims there from Saint Louis. He was on his way back east, hoping to find some work along the way at one of the forts—scouting, maybe, or providing game or food.

Now, he thought, he'd be lucky to survive. He'd

once known a man who'd been mauled by a grizzly, and the bear had scalped him.

"Did it better than any Injun could have," the old mountain man had told Fargo, taking off his hat to show him the white line of scar that ran along one side of his head. He still had his hair, or most of it, though it was a little patchy. "All the hair just flopped over to one side and hung there. I was lucky my partner was around. He kilt the bear and sewed my hair back on. Did a mighty nice job of it, too."

Fargo washed off as best he could in the stream. If the old mountain man had survived, so could he. The cold water sent shivers down his spine and then blasted him with pain when he washed the wounds.

He knew that a grizzly's claws were as likely to kill a man later on as they were when they first scored his flesh. Fargo had seen more than one wounded man come down with infections and fever from which they never recovered. He had some whiskey in his saddlebags if he could get back to his horse. He could pour the whiskey in the wound, and that would help, he hoped.

Fargo started back to where the big Ovaro stallion was waiting for him, watching the trees in case the bear returned.

Even if it did, however, there was nothing Fargo could have done against it. He was as weak as a newborn.

He got almost to the horse before he fell. He was barely able to get up, but somehow he did. He located the Ovaro and got the whiskey out of the saddlebags.

He knew that when he poured it on the wound, he was likely to pass out, but he didn't figure he had much choice. He uncorked the bottle and took a hefty swallow. Then, without hesitation, he doused the wound.

The pain was like being burned with hot irons. Fargo fell to his knees, his head spinning. The bottle fell from his hand, and he pitched forward. He raised his head once, but he lacked the strength to do so again.

No other series has this much historical action!

THE TRAILSMAN

Available wherever books are sold or at
penguin.com